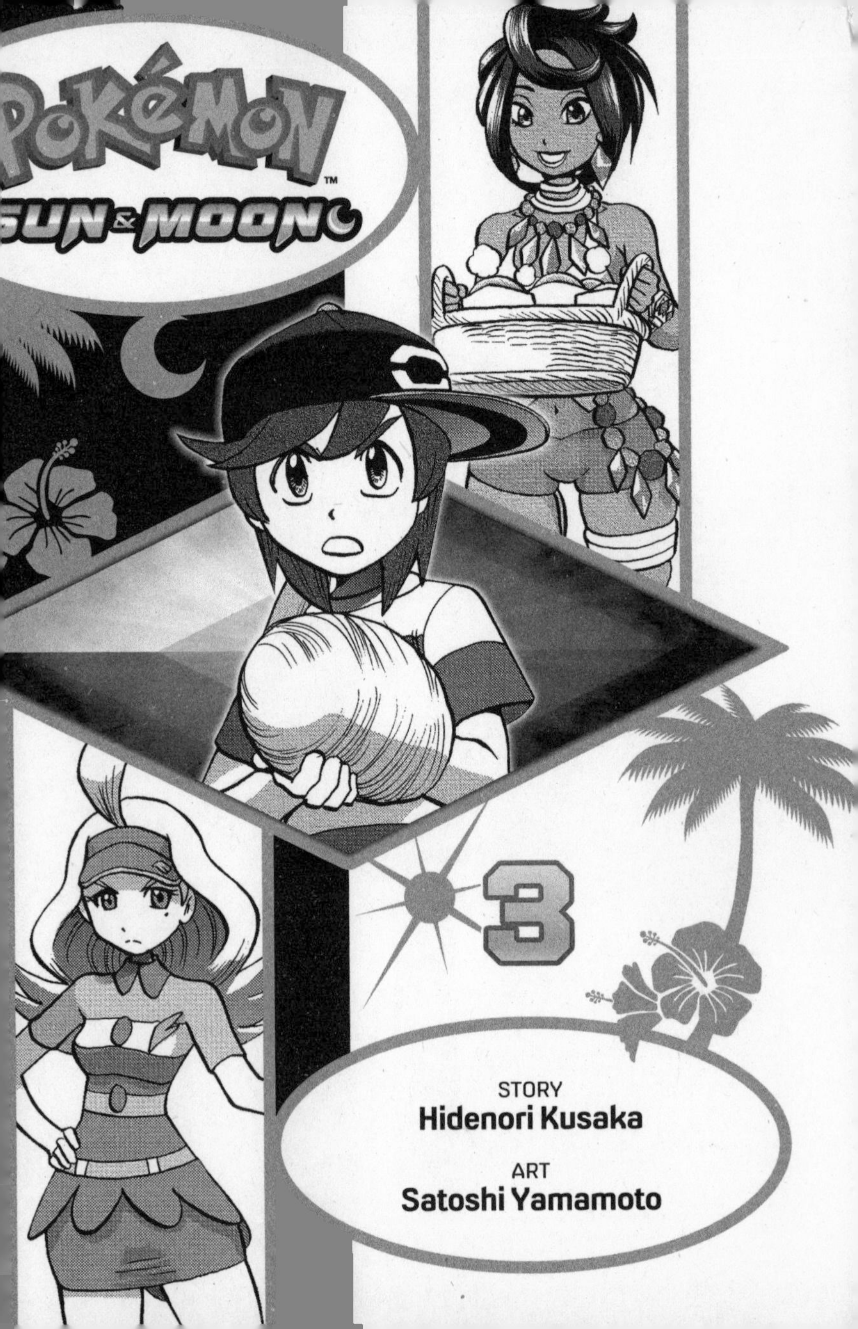
POKéMON™
SUN & MOON
3
STORY
Hidenori Kusaka
ART
Satoshi Yamamoto

Introduction

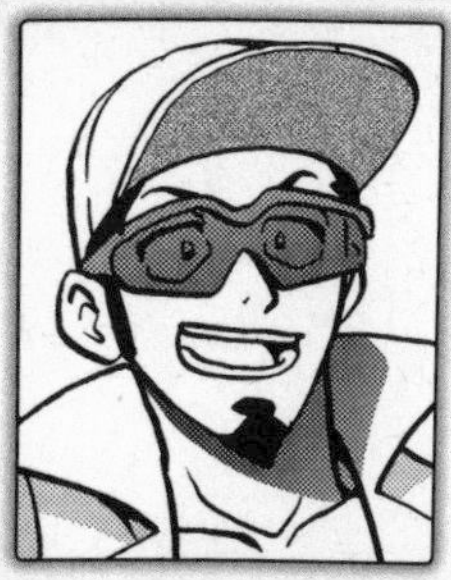

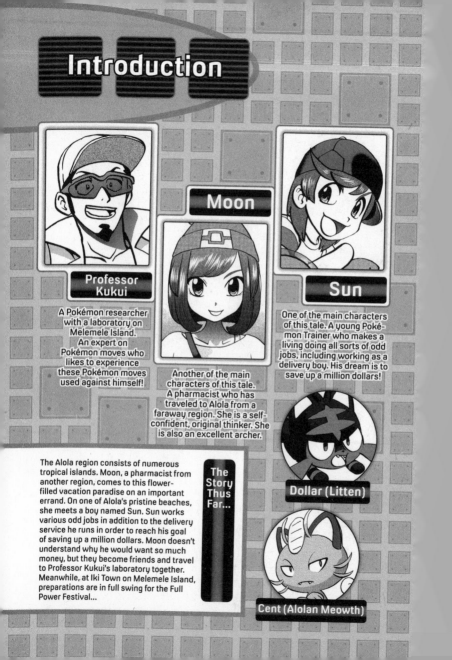

Professor Kukui

A Pokémon researcher with a laboratory on Melemele Island. An expert on Pokémon moves who likes to experience these Pokémon moves used against himself!

Moon

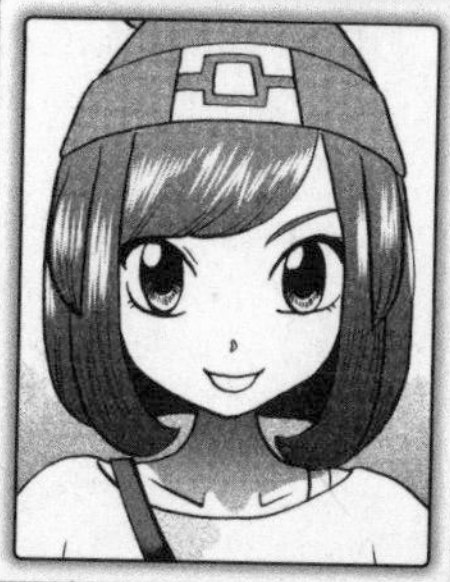

Another of the main characters of this tale. A pharmacist who has traveled to Alola from a faraway region. She is a self-confident, original thinker. She is also an excellent archer.

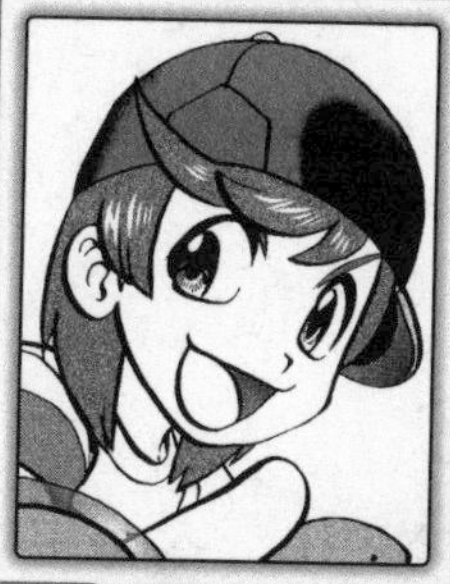

Sun

One of the main characters of this tale. A young Pokémon Trainer who makes a living doing all sorts of odd jobs, including working as a delivery boy. His dream is to save up a million dollars!

The Story Thus Far...

The Alola region consists of numerous tropical islands. Moon, a pharmacist from another region, comes to this flower-filled vacation paradise on an important errand. On one of Alola's pristine beaches, she meets a boy named Sun. Sun works various odd jobs in addition to the delivery service he runs in order to reach his goal of saving up a million dollars. Moon doesn't understand why he would want so much money, but they become friends and travel to Professor Kukui's laboratory together. Meanwhile, at Iki Town on Melemele Island, preparations are in full swing for the Full Power Festival...

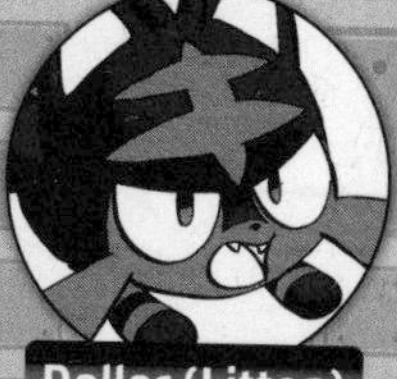

Dollar (Litten)

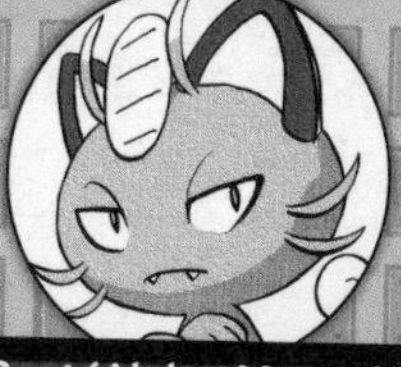

Cent (Alolan Meowth)

Character

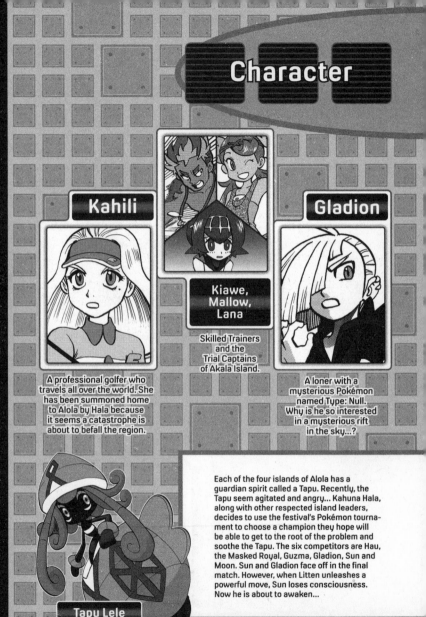

Kahili

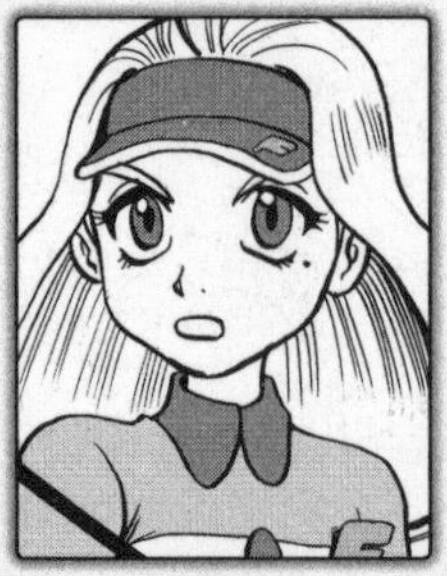

A professional golfer who travels all over the world. She has been summoned home to Alola by Hala because it seems a catastrophe is about to befall the region.

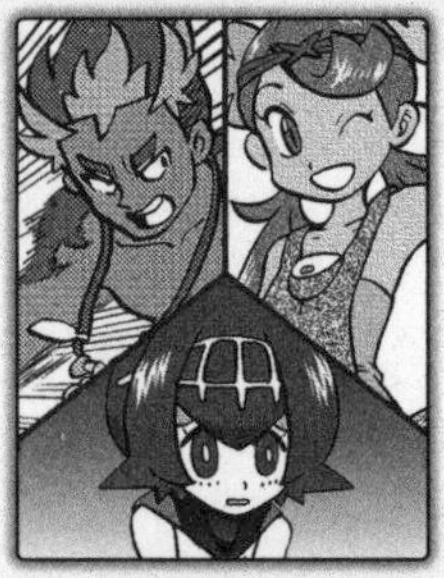

Kiawe, Mallow, Lana

Skilled Trainers and the Trial Captains of Akala Island.

Gladion

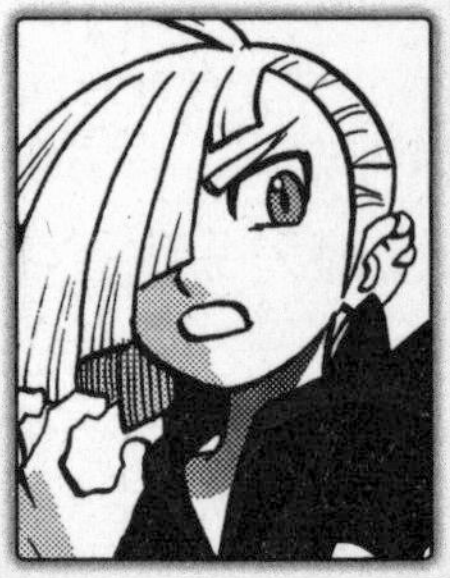

A loner with a mysterious Pokémon named Type: Null. Why is he so interested in a mysterious rift in the sky...?

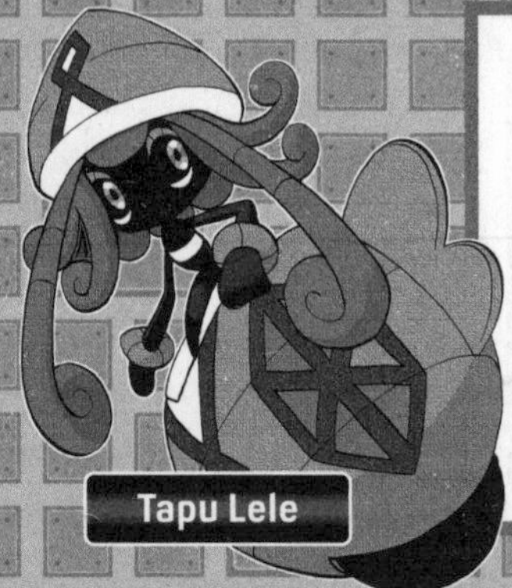

Tapu Lele

Each of the four islands of Alola has a guardian spirit called a Tapu. Recently, the Tapu seem agitated and angry... Kahuna Hala, along with other respected island leaders, decides to use the festival's Pokémon tournament to choose a champion they hope will be able to get to the root of the problem and soothe the Tapu. The six competitors are Hau, the Masked Royal, Guzma, Gladion, Sun and Moon. Sun and Gladion face off in the final match. However, when Litten unleashes a powerful move, Sun loses consciousness. Now he is about to awaken...

CONTENTS

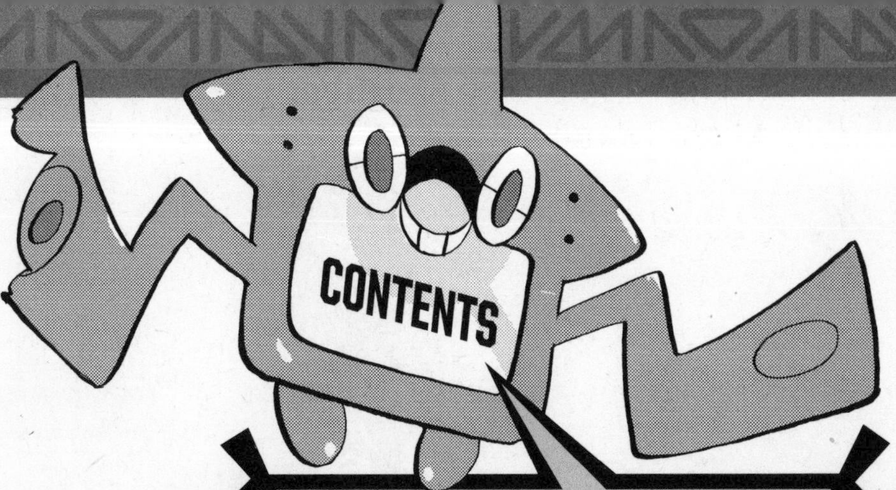

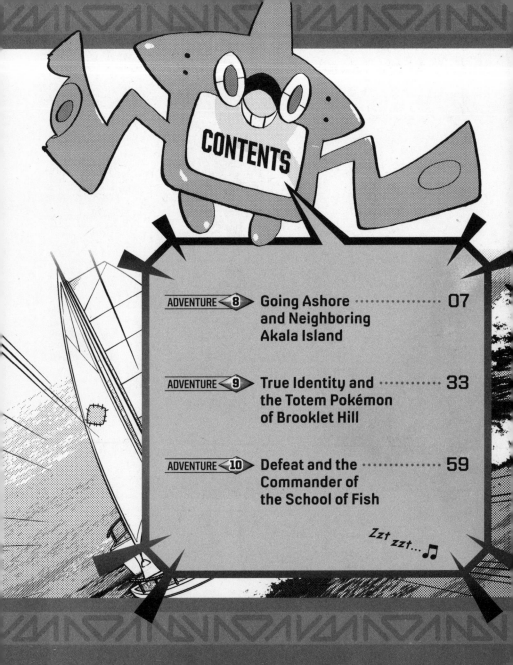

Zzt zzt...♫

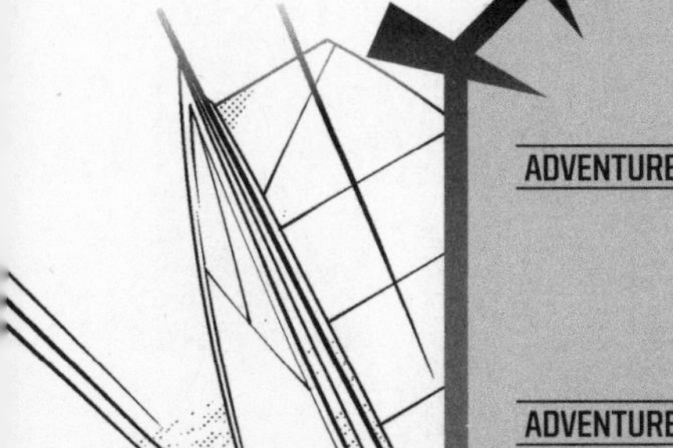

Adventure 8 Going Ashore and Neighboring Akala Island

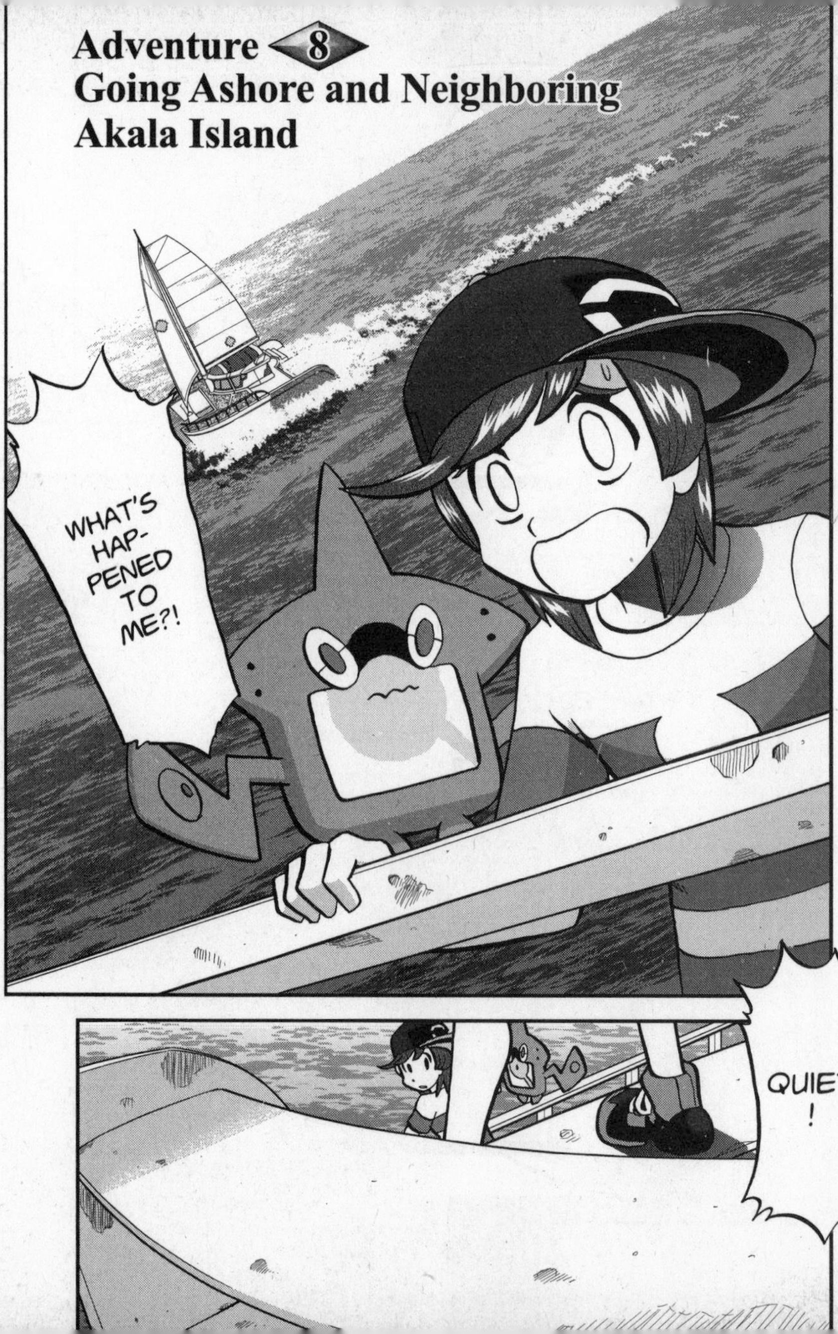
WHAT'S HAP-PENED TO ME?!
QUIET!

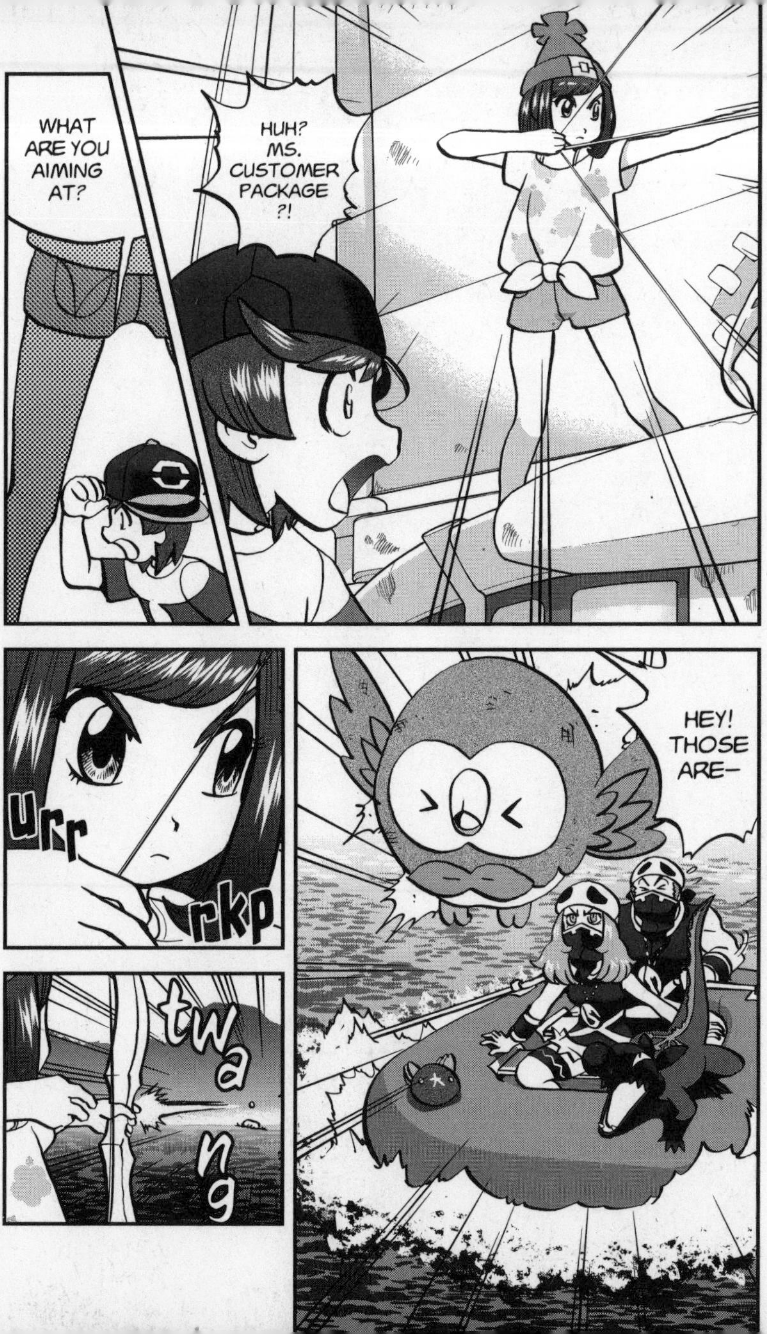
HUH? MS. CUSTOMER PACKAGE ?!
WHAT ARE YOU AIMING AT?
HEY! THOSE ARE—
urr
rkp
twang

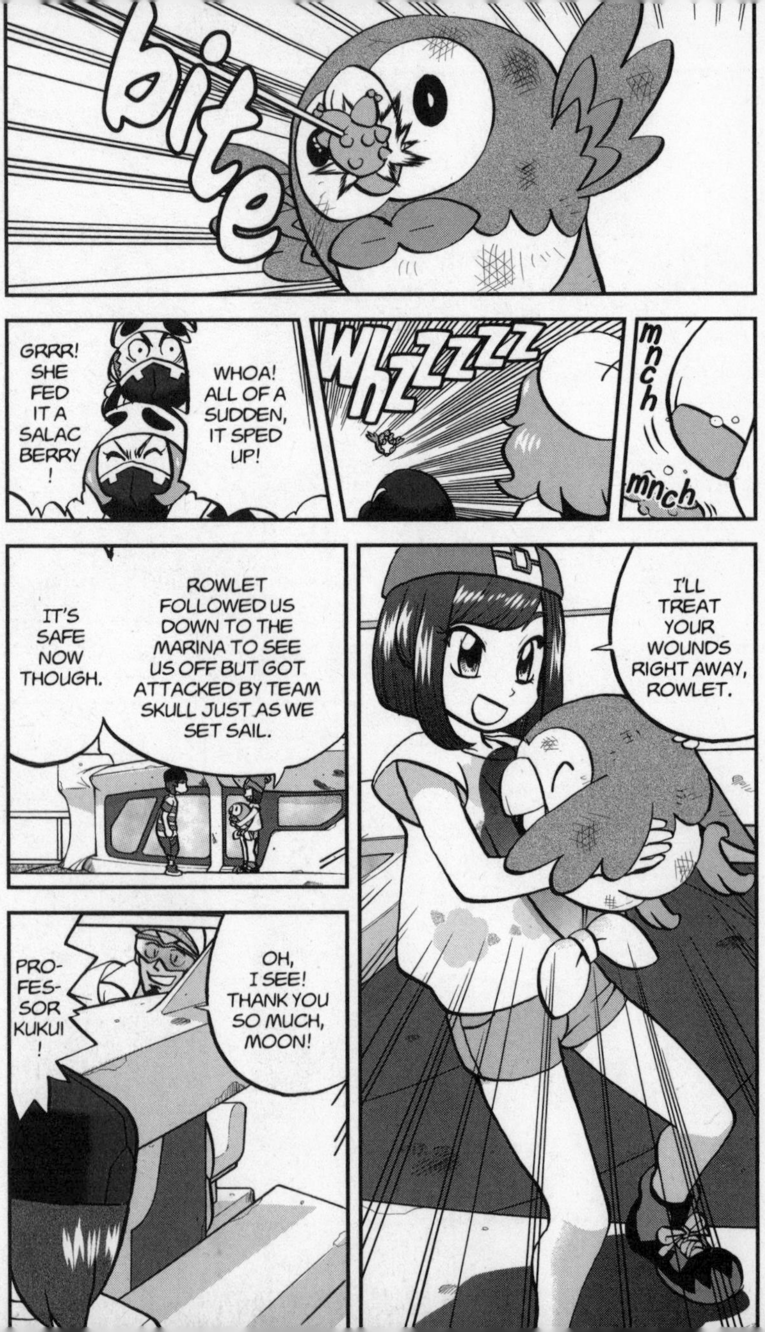
bite
mnch
mnch
whzzzzz
WHOA! ALL OF A SUDDEN, IT SPED UP!
GRRR! SHE FED IT A SALAC BERRY!
I'LL TREAT YOUR WOUNDS RIGHT AWAY, ROWLET.
ROWLET FOLLOWED US DOWN TO THE MARINA TO SEE US OFF BUT GOT ATTACKED BY TEAM SKULL JUST AS WE SET SAIL.
IT'S SAFE NOW THOUGH.
OH, I SEE! THANK YOU SO MUCH, MOON!
PRO-FES-SOR KUKUI!

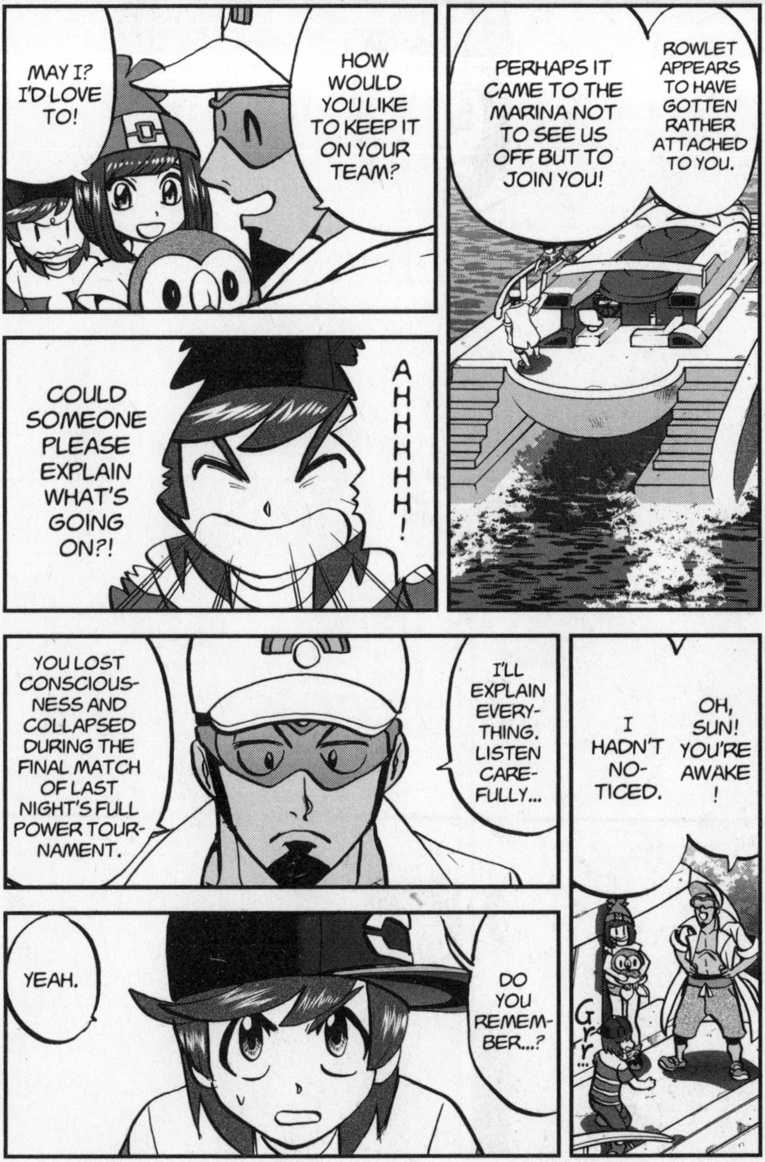
ROWLET APPEARS TO HAVE GOTTEN RATHER ATTACHED TO YOU.
PERHAPS IT CAME TO THE MARINA NOT TO SEE US OFF BUT TO JOIN YOU!
HOW WOULD YOU LIKE TO KEEP IT ON YOUR TEAM?
MAY I? I'D LOVE TO!
AHHHHH!
COULD SOMEONE PLEASE EXPLAIN WHAT'S GOING ON?!
OH, SUN! YOU'RE AWAKE!
I HADN'T NOTICED.
Grr...
I'LL EXPLAIN EVERYTHING. LISTEN CAREFULLY...
YOU LOST CONSCIOUSNESS AND COLLAPSED DURING THE FINAL MATCH OF LAST NIGHT'S FULL POWER TOURNAMENT.
DO YOU REMEMBER...?
YEAH.

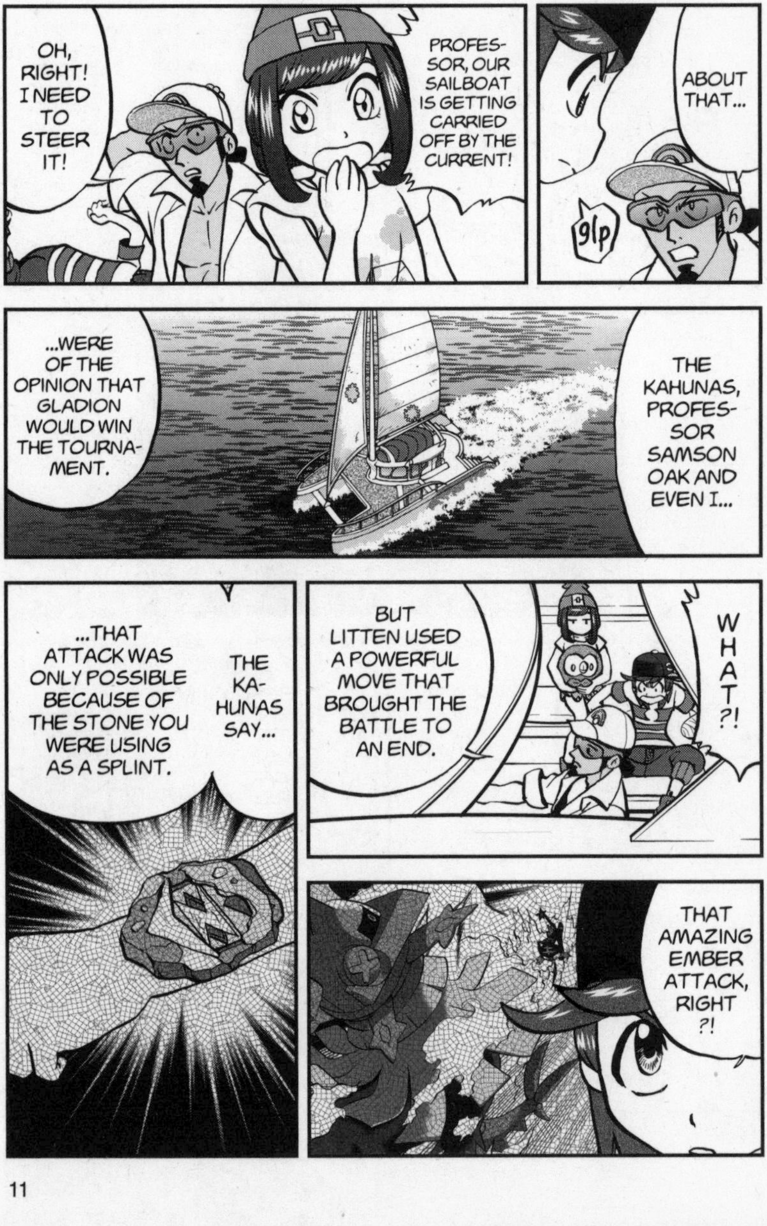
ABOUT THAT...
GLP
PROFESSOR, OUR SAILBOAT IS GETTING CARRIED OFF BY THE CURRENT!
OH, RIGHT! I NEED TO STEER IT!
THE KAHUNAS, PROFESSOR SAMSON OAK AND EVEN I...
...WERE OF THE OPINION THAT GLADION WOULD WIN THE TOURNAMENT.
WHAT?!
BUT LITTEN USED A POWERFUL MOVE THAT BROUGHT THE BATTLE TO AN END.
THAT AMAZING EMBER ATTACK, RIGHT?!
THE KAHUNAS SAY...
...THAT ATTACK WAS ONLY POSSIBLE BECAUSE OF THE STONE YOU WERE USING AS A SPLINT.

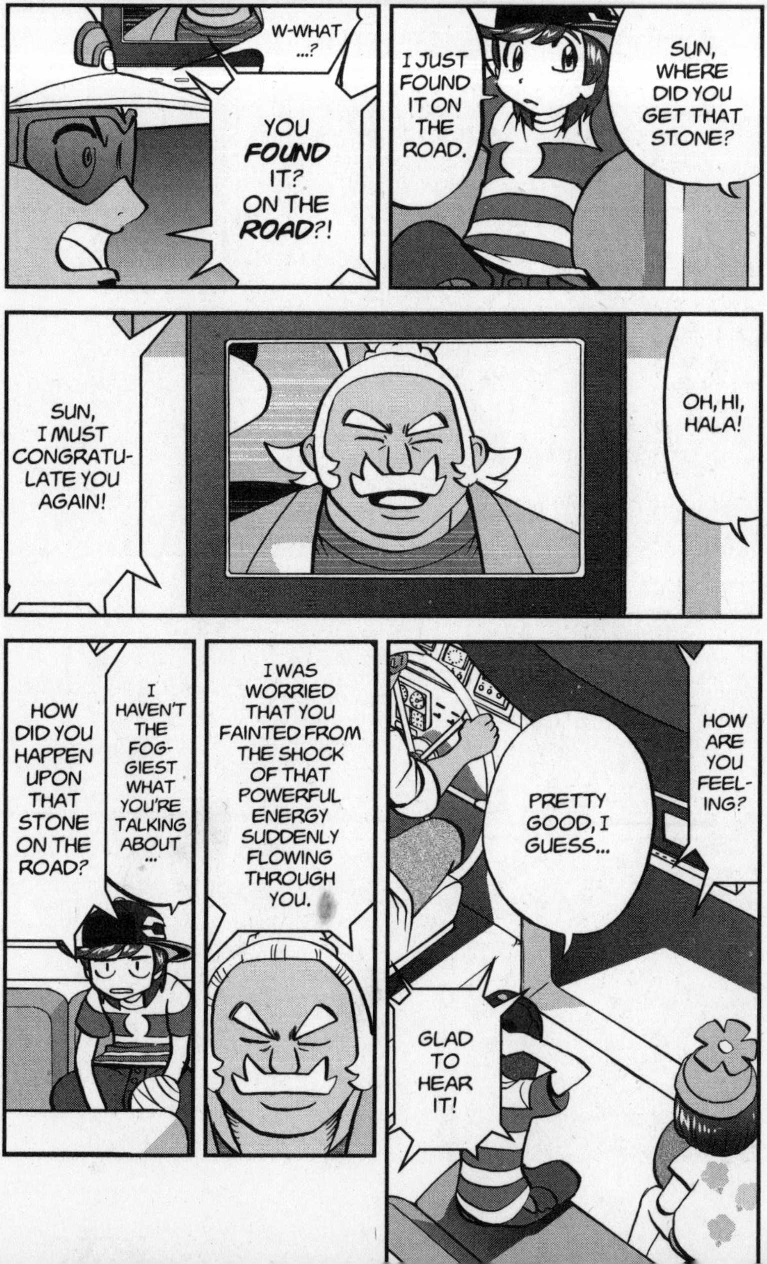

SUN, WHERE DID YOU GET THAT STONE?
I JUST FOUND IT ON THE ROAD.
W-WHAT ...?
YOU **FOUND** IT? ON THE **ROAD**?!
OH, HI, HALA!
SUN, I MUST CONGRATULATE YOU AGAIN!
HOW ARE YOU FEELING?
PRETTY GOOD, I GUESS...
GLAD TO HEAR IT!
I WAS WORRIED THAT YOU FAINTED FROM THE SHOCK OF THAT POWERFUL ENERGY SUDDENLY FLOWING THROUGH YOU.
HOW DID YOU HAPPEN UPON THAT STONE ON THE ROAD?
I HAVEN'T THE FOGGIEST WHAT YOU'RE TALKING ABOUT...

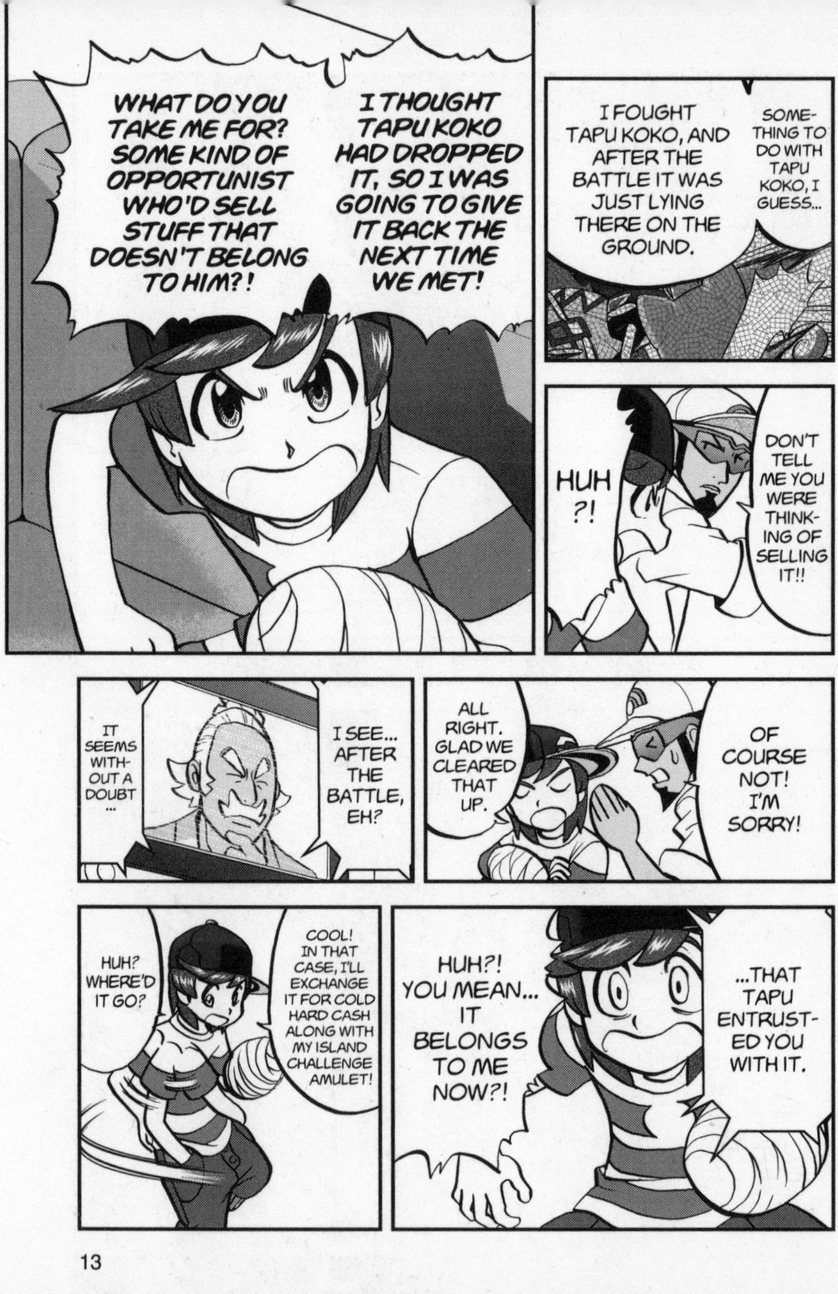
SOMETHING TO DO WITH TAPU KOKO, I GUESS...
I FOUGHT TAPU KOKO, AND AFTER THE BATTLE IT WAS JUST LYING THERE ON THE GROUND.
DON'T TELL ME YOU WERE THINKING OF SELLING IT!!
HUH ?!
I THOUGHT TAPU KOKO HAD DROPPED IT, SO I WAS GOING TO GIVE IT BACK THE NEXT TIME WE MET!
WHAT DO YOU TAKE ME FOR? SOME KIND OF OPPORTUNIST WHO'D SELL STUFF THAT DOESN'T BELONG TO HIM?!
OF COURSE NOT! I'M SORRY!
ALL RIGHT. GLAD WE CLEARED THAT UP.
I SEE... AFTER THE BATTLE, EH?
IT SEEMS WITHOUT A DOUBT...
...THAT TAPU ENTRUSTED YOU WITH IT.
HUH?! YOU MEAN... IT BELONGS TO ME NOW?!
COOL! IN THAT CASE, I'LL EXCHANGE IT FOR COLD HARD CASH ALONG WITH MY ISLAND CHALLENGE AMULET!
HUH? WHERE'D IT GO?

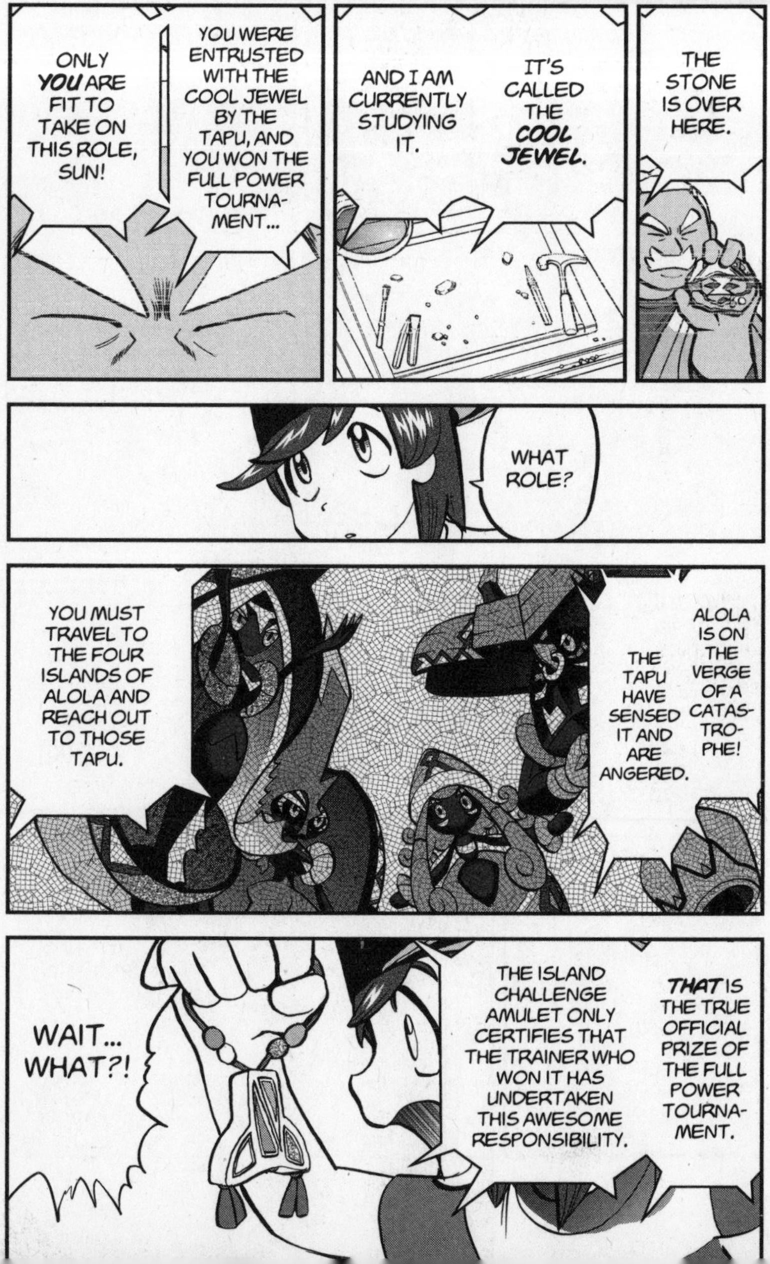
THE STONE IS OVER HERE.
IT'S CALLED THE COOL JEWEL.
AND I AM CURRENTLY STUDYING IT.
YOU WERE ENTRUSTED WITH THE COOL JEWEL BY THE TAPU, AND YOU WON THE FULL POWER TOURNAMENT...
ONLY YOU ARE FIT TO TAKE ON THIS ROLE, SUN!
WHAT ROLE?
ALOLA IS ON THE VERGE OF A CATASTROPHE!
THE TAPU HAVE SENSED IT AND ARE ANGERED.
YOU MUST TRAVEL TO THE FOUR ISLANDS OF ALOLA AND REACH OUT TO THOSE TAPU.
THAT IS THE TRUE OFFICIAL PRIZE OF THE FULL POWER TOURNAMENT.
THE ISLAND CHALLENGE AMULET ONLY CERTIFIES THAT THE TRAINER WHO WON IT HAS UNDERTAKEN THIS AWESOME RESPONSIBILITY.
WAIT... WHAT?!

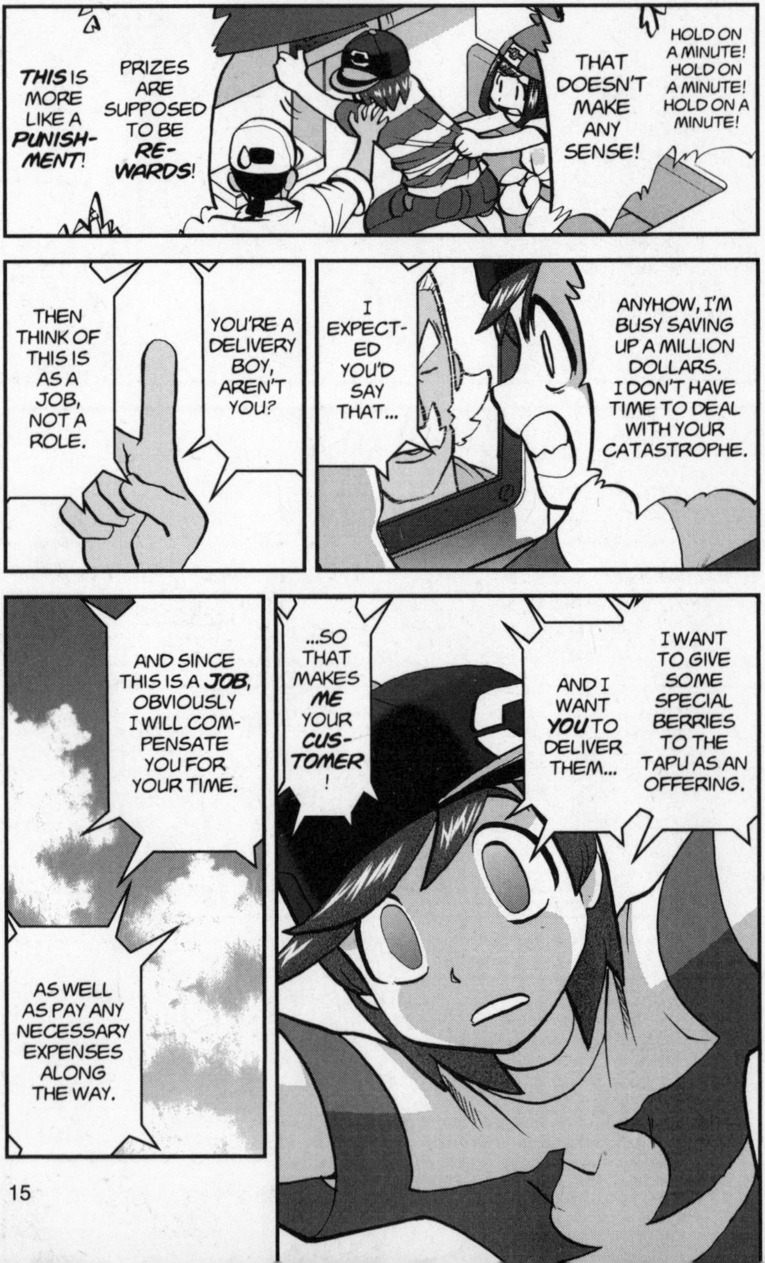
HOLD ON A MINUTE! HOLD ON A MINUTE! HOLD ON A MINUTE!
THAT DOESN'T MAKE ANY SENSE!
PRIZES ARE SUPPOSED TO BE REWARDS!
THIS IS MORE LIKE A PUNISHMENT!
ANYHOW, I'M BUSY SAVING UP A MILLION DOLLARS. I DON'T HAVE TIME TO DEAL WITH YOUR CATASTROPHE.
I EXPECTED YOU'D SAY THAT...
YOU'RE A DELIVERY BOY, AREN'T YOU?
THEN THINK OF THIS IS AS A JOB, NOT A ROLE.
I WANT TO GIVE SOME SPECIAL BERRIES TO THE TAPU AS AN OFFERING.
AND I WANT YOU TO DELIVER THEM...
...SO THAT MAKES ME YOUR CUSTOMER!
AND SINCE THIS IS A JOB, OBVIOUSLY I WILL COMPENSATE YOU FOR YOUR TIME.
AS WELL AS PAY ANY NECESSARY EXPENSES ALONG THE WAY.

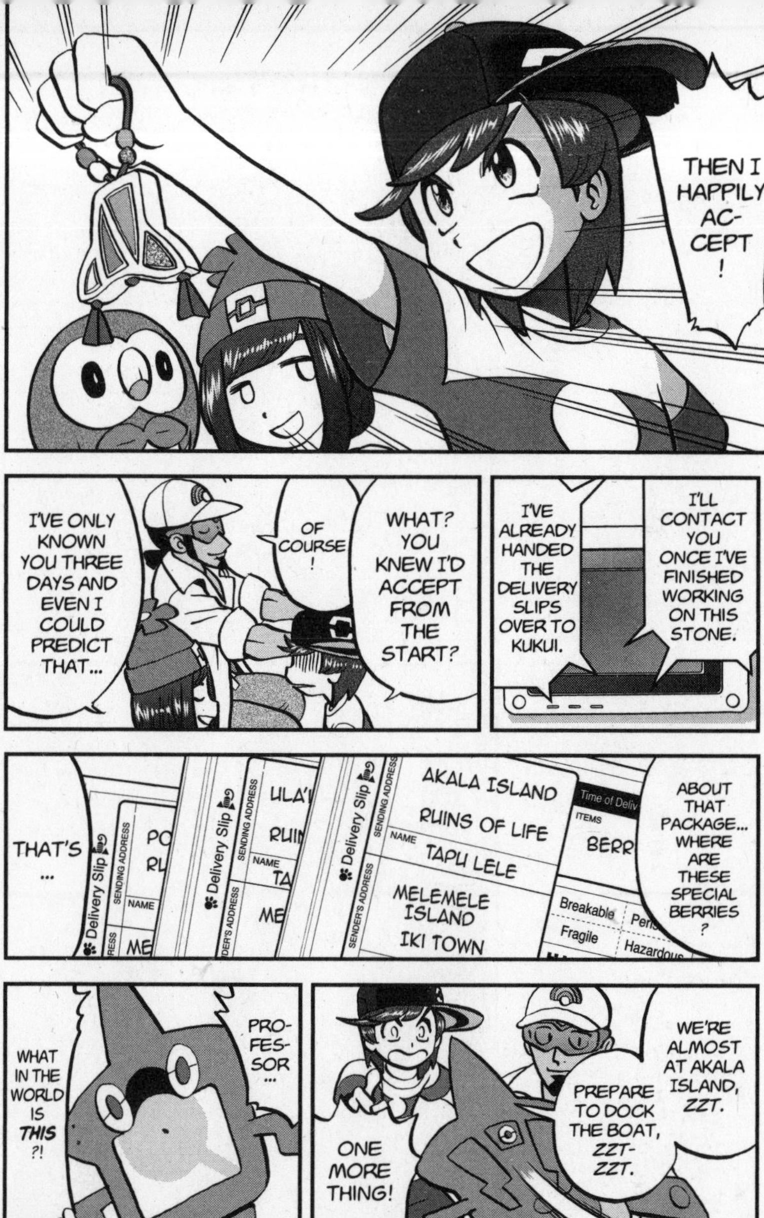
THEN I HAPPILY AC-CEPT!
I'LL CONTACT YOU ONCE I'VE FINISHED WORKING ON THIS STONE.
I'VE ALREADY HANDED THE DELIVERY SLIPS OVER TO KUKUI.
WHAT? YOU KNEW I'D ACCEPT FROM THE START?
OF COURSE!
I'VE ONLY KNOWN YOU THREE DAYS AND EVEN I COULD PREDICT THAT...
ABOUT THAT PACKAGE... WHERE ARE THESE SPECIAL BERRIES?
ITEMS
Breakable
Fragile
Delivery Slip
SENDING ADDRESS
AKALA ISLAND
RUINS OF LIFE
NAME
TAPU LELE
SENDER'S ADDRESS
MELEMELE ISLAND
IKI TOWN
THAT'S...
WE'RE ALMOST AT AKALA ISLAND, ZZT.
PREPARE TO DOCK THE BOAT, ZZT-ZZT.
ONE MORE THING!
PRO-FES-SOR...
WHAT IN THE WORLD IS THIS?!

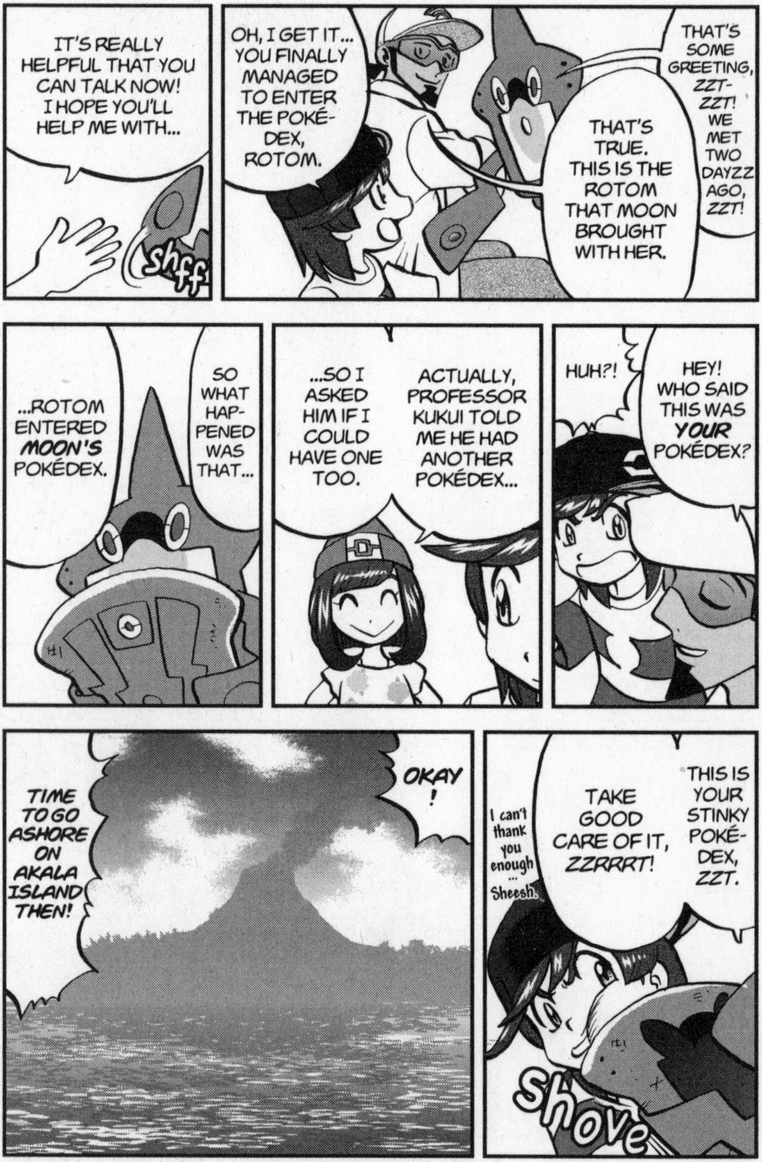
THAT'S SOME GREETING, ZZT-ZZT! WE MET TWO DAYZZ AGO, ZZT!
THAT'S TRUE. THIS IS THE ROTOM THAT MOON BROUGHT WITH HER.
OH, I GET IT... YOU FINALLY MANAGED TO ENTER THE POKÉ-DEX, ROTOM.
IT'S REALLY HELPFUL THAT YOU CAN TALK NOW! I HOPE YOU'LL HELP ME WITH...
shff
HEY! WHO SAID THIS WAS **YOUR** POKÉDEX?
HUH?!
ACTUALLY, PROFESSOR KUKUI TOLD ME HE HAD ANOTHER POKÉDEX...
...SO I ASKED HIM IF I COULD HAVE ONE TOO.
SO WHAT HAP-PENED WAS THAT...
...ROTOM ENTERED **MOON'S** POKÉDEX.
THIS IS YOUR STINKY POKÉ-DEX, ZZT.
TAKE GOOD CARE OF IT, ZZRRRT!
I can't thank you enough... Sheesh.
Shove
OKAY!
TIME TO GO ASHORE ON AKALA ISLAND THEN!

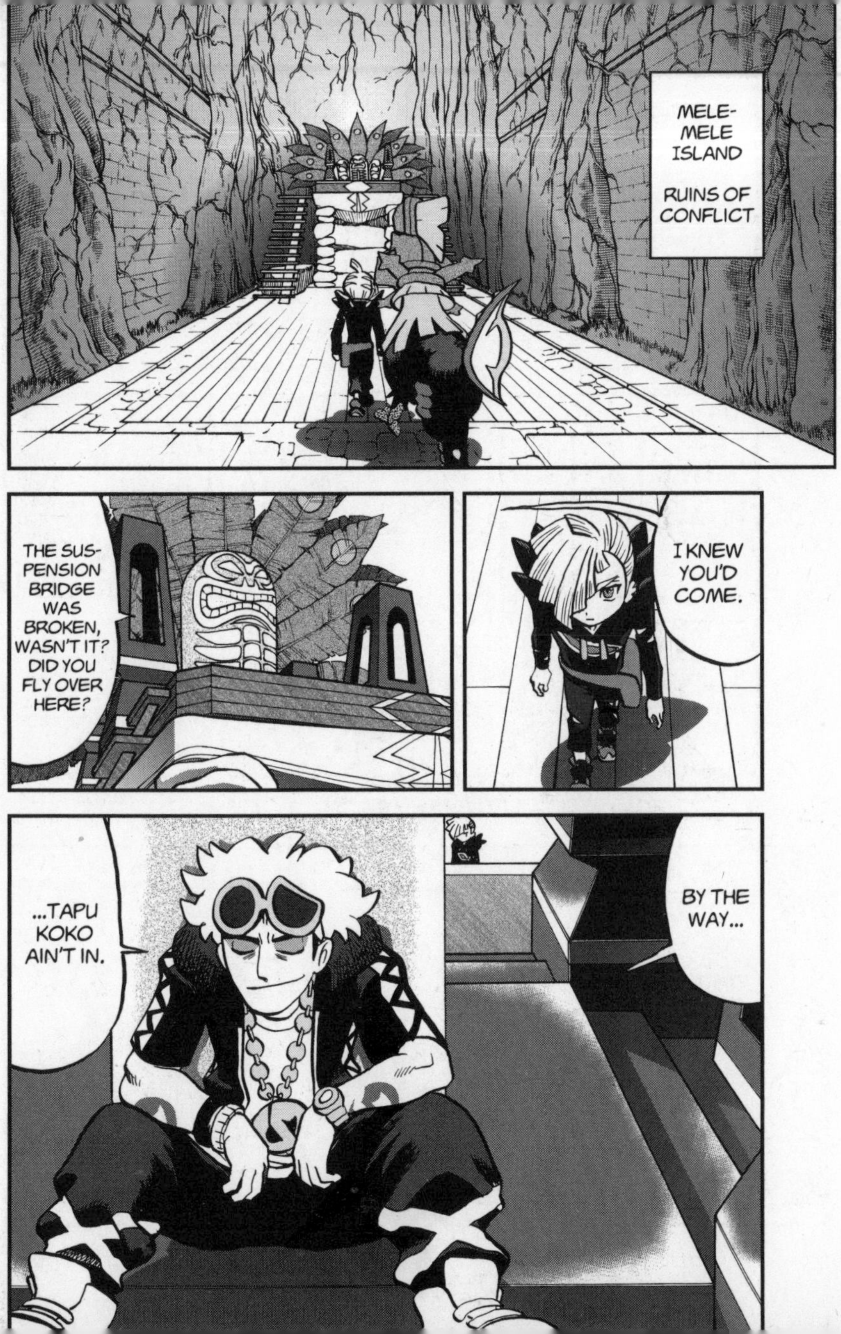
MELE-MELE ISLAND
RUINS OF CONFLICT
I KNEW YOU'D COME.
THE SUS-PENSION BRIDGE WAS BROKEN, WASN'T IT? DID YOU FLY OVER HERE?
BY THE WAY...
...TAPU KOKO AIN'T IN.

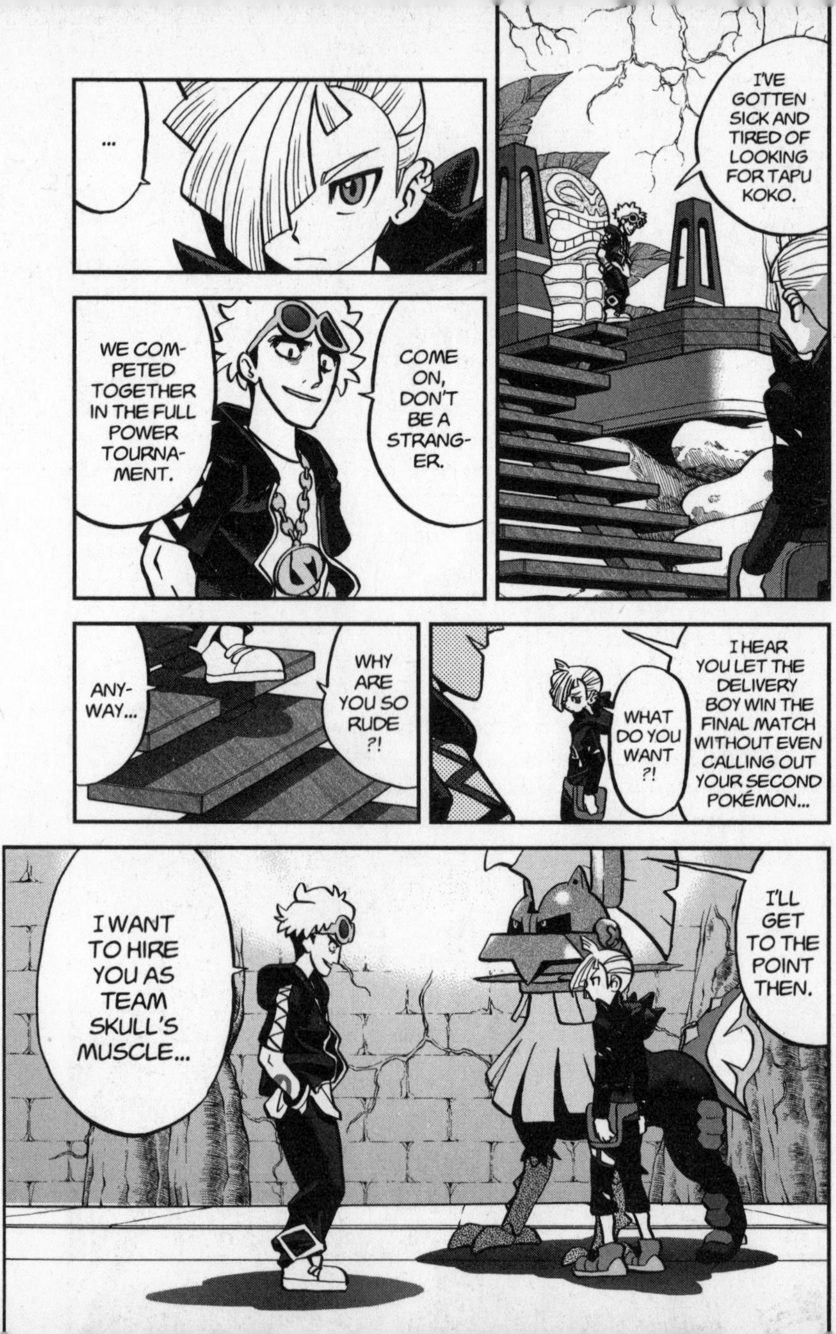
I'VE GOTTEN SICK AND TIRED OF LOOKING FOR TAPU KOKO.
...
COME ON, DON'T BE A STRANGER.
WE COMPETED TOGETHER IN THE FULL POWER TOURNAMENT.
I HEAR YOU LET THE DELIVERY BOY WIN THE FINAL MATCH WITHOUT EVEN CALLING OUT YOUR SECOND POKÉMON...
WHAT DO YOU WANT ?!
WHY ARE YOU SO RUDE ?!
ANYWAY...
I'LL GET TO THE POINT THEN.
I WANT TO HIRE YOU AS TEAM SKULL'S MUSCLE...

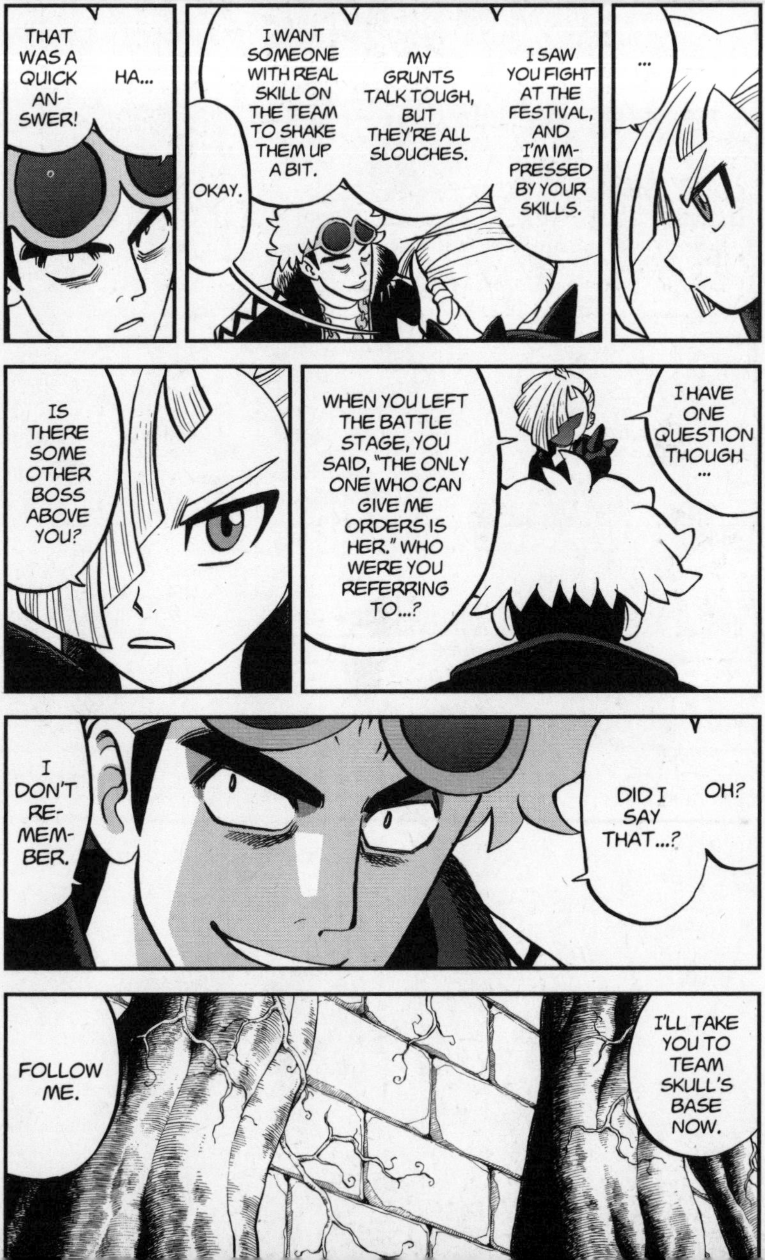
...
I SAW YOU FIGHT AT THE FESTIVAL, AND I'M IMPRESSED BY YOUR SKILLS.
MY GRUNTS TALK TOUGH, BUT THEY'RE ALL SLOUCHES.
I WANT SOMEONE WITH REAL SKILL ON THE TEAM TO SHAKE THEM UP A BIT.
OKAY.
HA...
THAT WAS A QUICK ANSWER!
I HAVE ONE QUESTION THOUGH...
WHEN YOU LEFT THE BATTLE STAGE, YOU SAID, "THE ONLY ONE WHO CAN GIVE ME ORDERS IS HER." WHO WERE YOU REFERRING TO...?
IS THERE SOME OTHER BOSS ABOVE YOU?
OH?
DID I SAY THAT...?
I DON'T REMEMBER.
I'LL TAKE YOU TO TEAM SKULL'S BASE NOW.
FOLLOW ME.

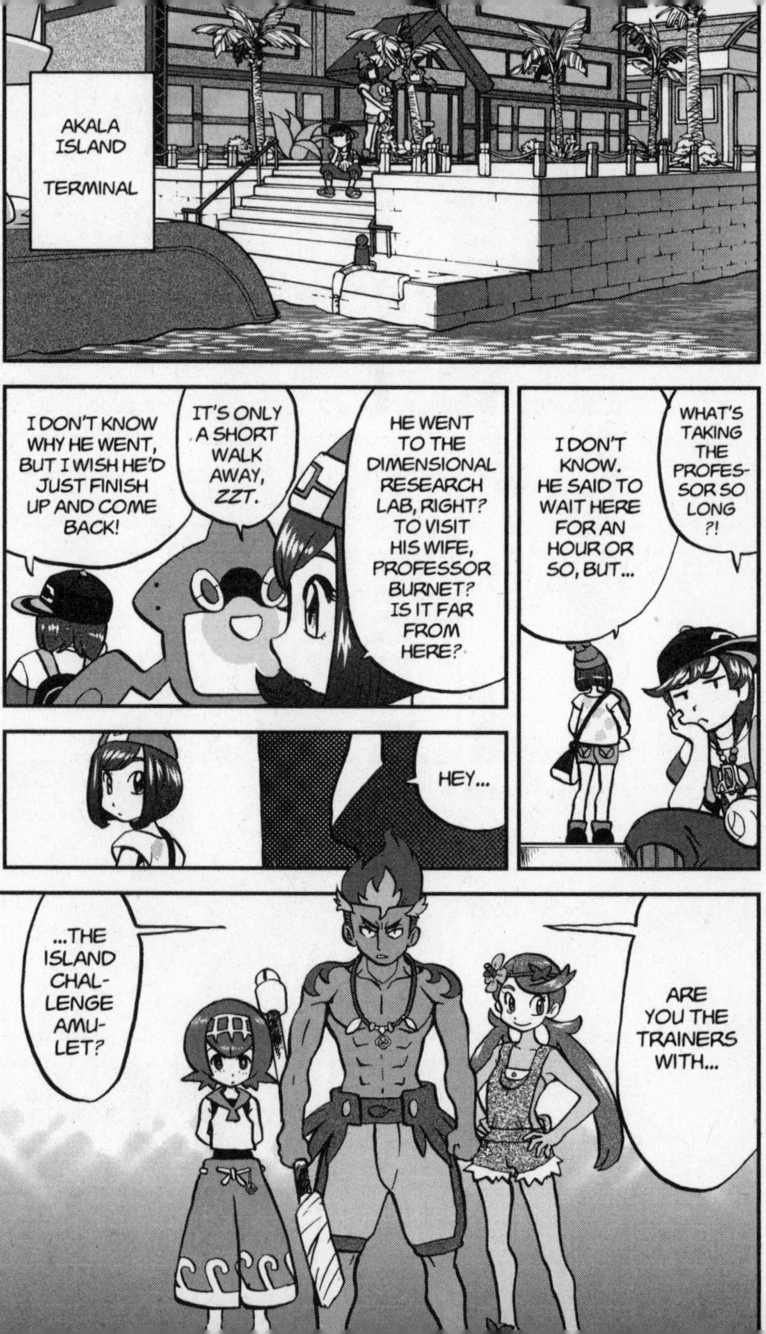
AKALA ISLAND
TERMINAL
WHAT'S TAKING THE PROFES-SOR SO LONG?!
I DON'T KNOW. HE SAID TO WAIT HERE FOR AN HOUR OR SO, BUT...
HE WENT TO THE DIMENSIONAL RESEARCH LAB, RIGHT? TO VISIT HIS WIFE, PROFESSOR BURNET? IS IT FAR FROM HERE?
IT'S ONLY A SHORT WALK AWAY, ZZT.
I DON'T KNOW WHY HE WENT, BUT I WISH HE'D JUST FINISH UP AND COME BACK!
HEY...
ARE YOU THE TRAINERS WITH...
...THE ISLAND CHAL-LENGE AMU-LET?

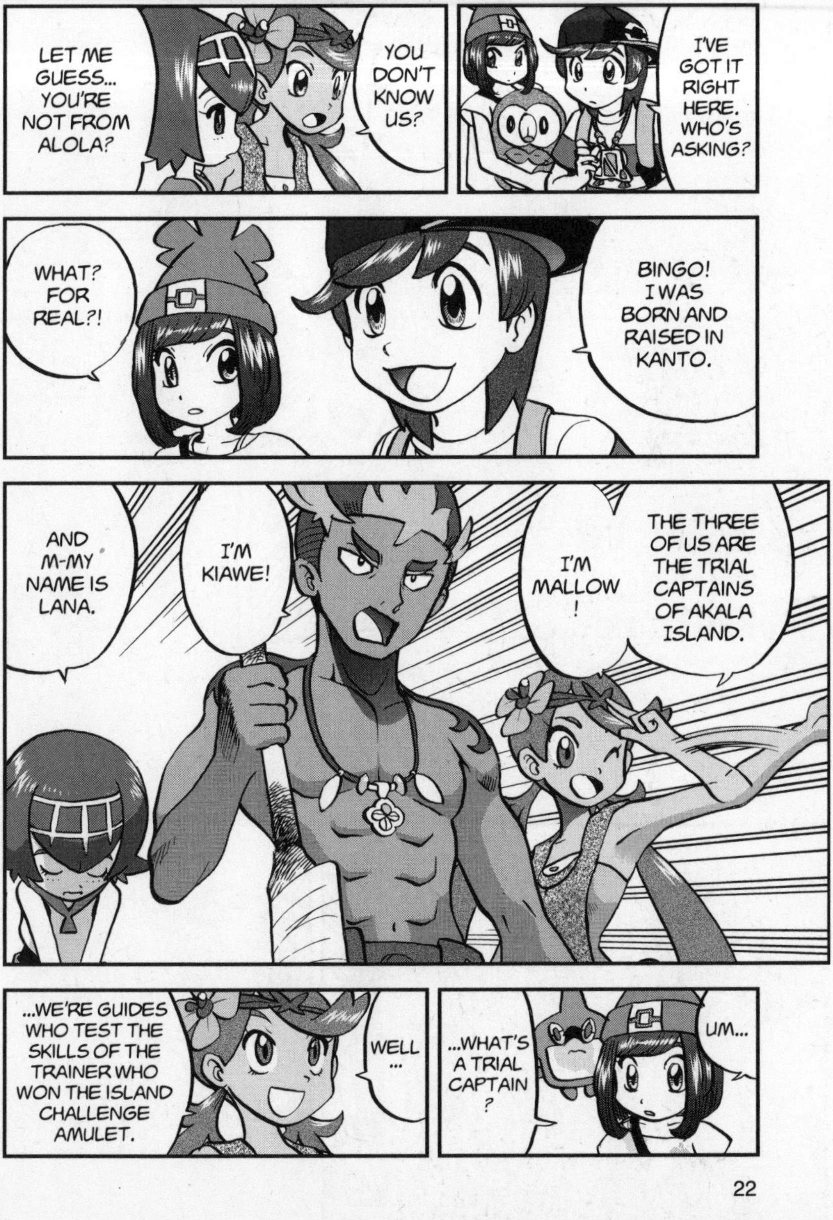
I'VE GOT IT RIGHT HERE. WHO'S ASKING?
YOU DON'T KNOW US?
LET ME GUESS... YOU'RE NOT FROM ALOLA?
BINGO! I WAS BORN AND RAISED IN KANTO.
WHAT? FOR REAL?!
THE THREE OF US ARE THE TRIAL CAPTAINS OF AKALA ISLAND.
I'M MALLOW!
I'M KIAWE!
AND M-MY NAME IS LANA.
UM...
...WHAT'S A TRIAL CAPTAIN?
WELL...
...WE'RE GUIDES WHO TEST THE SKILLS OF THE TRAINER WHO WON THE ISLAND CHALLENGE AMULET.

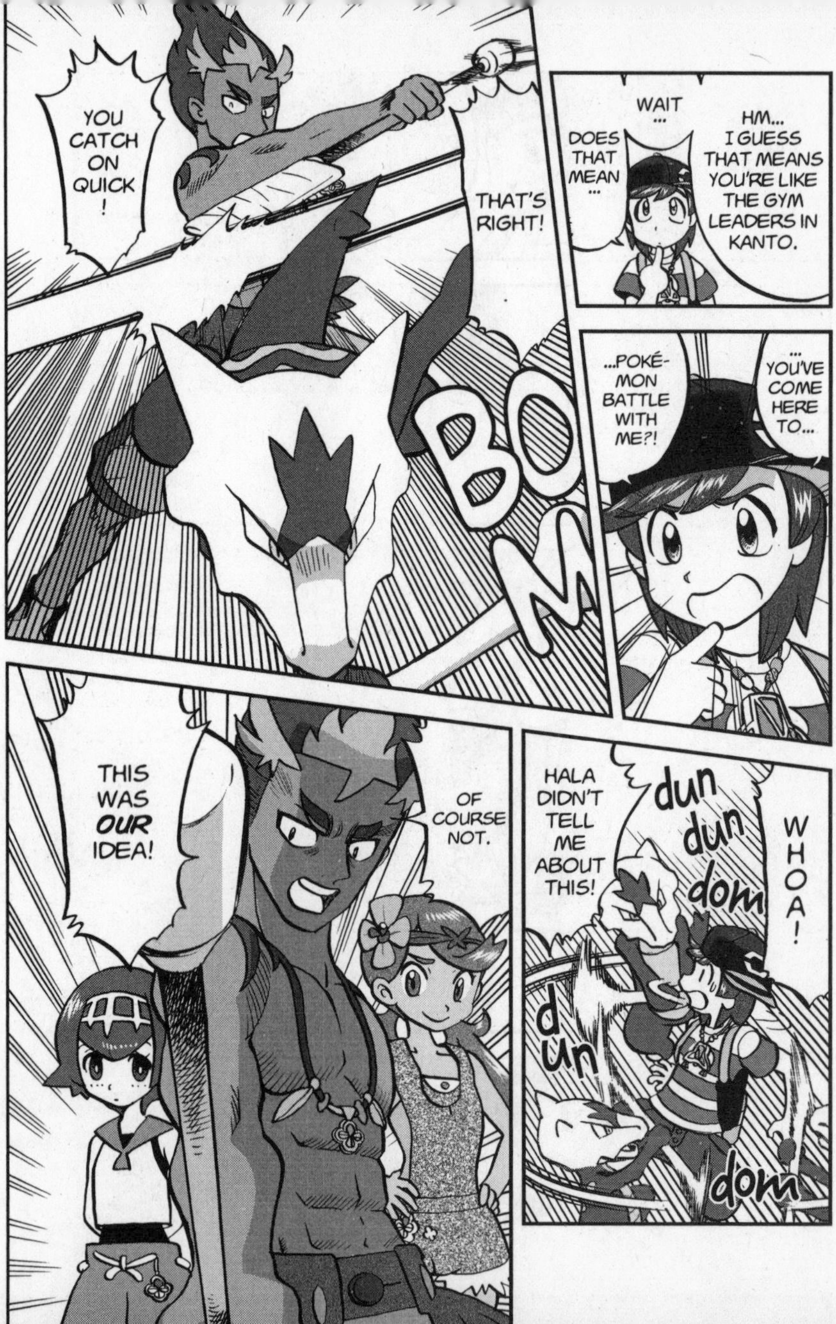
HM... I GUESS THAT MEANS YOU'RE LIKE THE GYM LEADERS IN KANTO.
WAIT ... DOES THAT MEAN ...
... YOU'VE COME HERE TO...
...POKÉ-MON BATTLE WITH ME?!
THAT'S RIGHT!
YOU CATCH ON QUICK!
BOOM
WHOA!
dun dun dom
HALA DIDN'T TELL ME ABOUT THIS!
dun dom
OF COURSE NOT.
THIS WAS ***OUR*** IDEA!

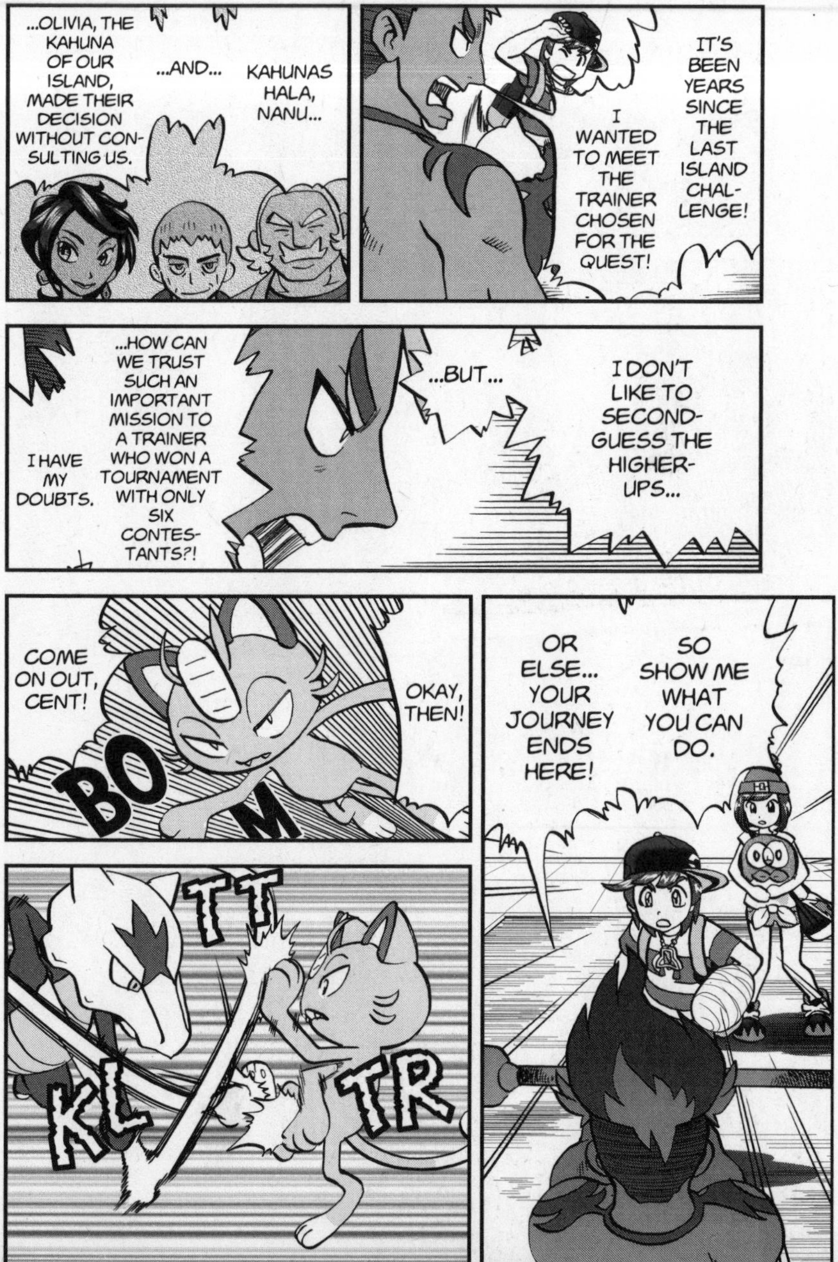
IT'S BEEN YEARS SINCE THE LAST ISLAND CHAL-LENGE!
I WANTED TO MEET THE TRAINER CHOSEN FOR THE QUEST!
KAHUNAS HALA, NANU...
...AND...
...OLIVIA, THE KAHUNA OF OUR ISLAND, MADE THEIR DECISION WITHOUT CON-SULTING US.
I DON'T LIKE TO SECOND-GUESS THE HIGHER-UPS...
...BUT...
...HOW CAN WE TRUST SUCH AN IMPORTANT MISSION TO A TRAINER WHO WON A TOURNAMENT WITH ONLY SIX CONTES-TANTS?!
I HAVE MY DOUBTS.
SO SHOW ME WHAT YOU CAN DO.
OR ELSE... YOUR JOURNEY ENDS HERE!
OKAY, THEN!
COME ON OUT, CENT!
BOOM
TT
TR
KL

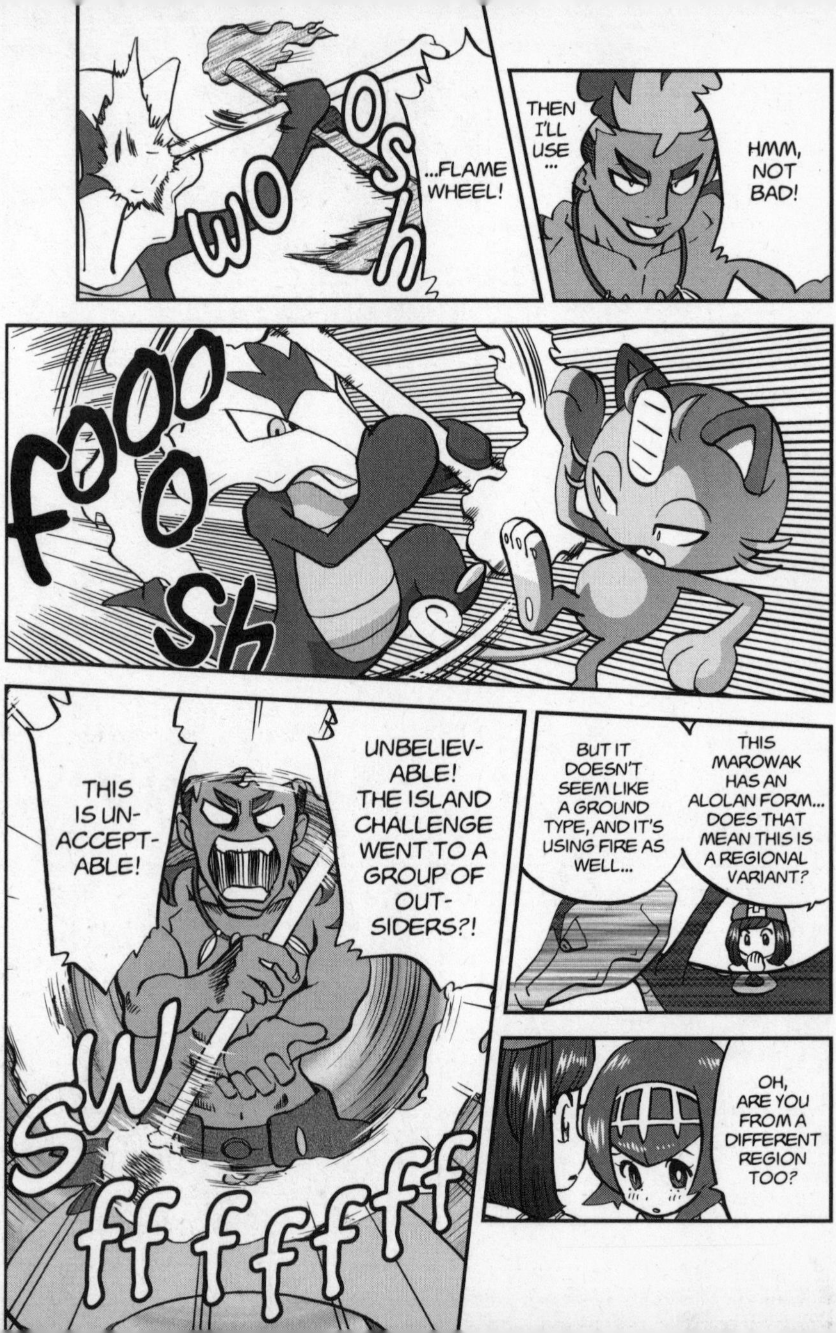

HMM, NOT BAD!
THEN I'LL USE ...
...FLAME WHEEL!
WOOSH
FOOOOOSH
THIS MAROWAK HAS AN ALOLAN FORM... DOES THAT MEAN THIS IS A REGIONAL VARIANT?
BUT IT DOESN'T SEEM LIKE A GROUND TYPE, AND IT'S USING FIRE AS WELL...
OH, ARE YOU FROM A DIFFERENT REGION TOO?
UNBELIEV-ABLE! THE ISLAND CHALLENGE WENT TO A GROUP OF OUT-SIDERS?!
THIS IS UN-ACCEPT-ABLE!
SWFFFFFFFF

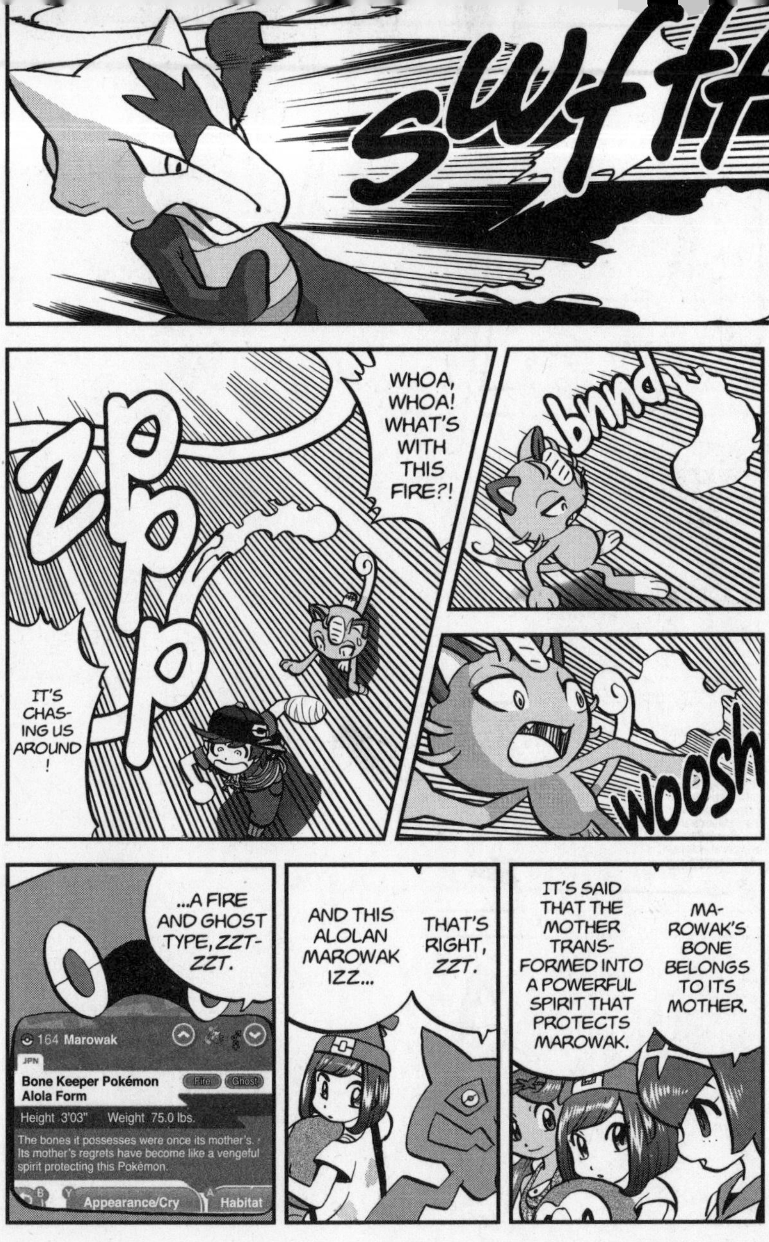
swfff
bnnd
WHOA, WHOA! WHAT'S WITH THIS FIRE?!
woosh
zppp
IT'S CHAS-ING US AROUND!
MA-ROWAK'S BONE BELONGS TO ITS MOTHER.
IT'S SAID THAT THE MOTHER TRANS-FORMED INTO A POWERFUL SPIRIT THAT PROTECTS MAROWAK.
THAT'S RIGHT, ZZT.
AND THIS ALOLAN MAROWAK IZZ...
...A FIRE AND GHOST TYPE, ZZT-ZZT.
164 Marowak
JPN
Bone Keeper Pokémon
Alola Form
Fire
Ghost
Height 3'03"
Weight 75.0 lbs.
The bones it possesses were once its mother's. Its mother's regrets have become like a vengeful spirit protecting this Pokémon.
B
Y
Appearance/Cry
A
Habitat

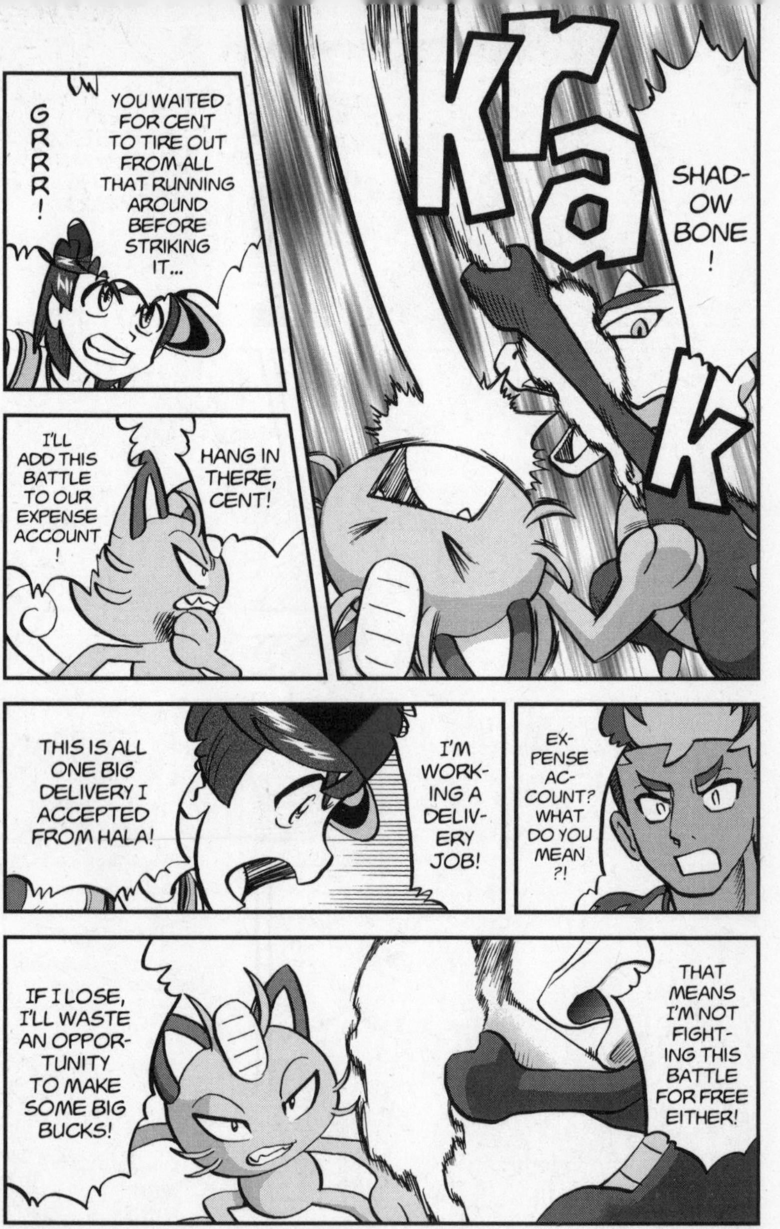
KRAAK
SHADOW BONE!
YOU WAITED FOR CENT TO TIRE OUT FROM ALL THAT RUNNING AROUND BEFORE STRIKING IT...
GRRR!
HANG IN THERE, CENT!
I'LL ADD THIS BATTLE TO OUR EXPENSE ACCOUNT!
EXPENSE ACCOUNT? WHAT DO YOU MEAN?!
I'M WORKING A DELIVERY JOB!
THIS IS ALL ONE BIG DELIVERY I ACCEPTED FROM HALA!
THAT MEANS I'M NOT FIGHTING THIS BATTLE FOR FREE EITHER!
IF I LOSE, I'LL WASTE AN OPPORTUNITY TO MAKE SOME BIG BUCKS!

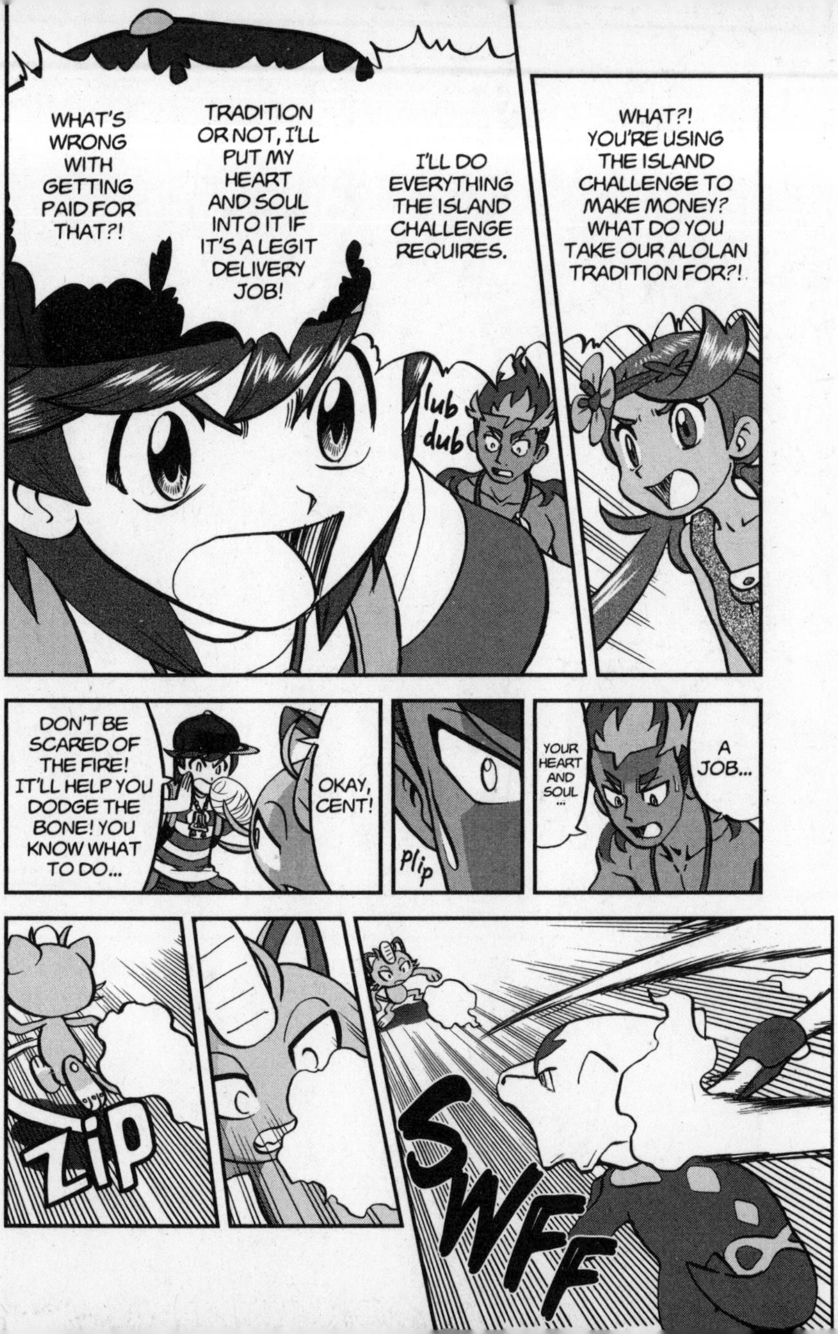
WHAT?! YOU'RE USING THE ISLAND CHALLENGE TO MAKE MONEY? WHAT DO YOU TAKE OUR ALOLAN TRADITION FOR?!
I'LL DO EVERYTHING THE ISLAND CHALLENGE REQUIRES.
TRADITION OR NOT, I'LL PUT MY HEART AND SOUL INTO IT IF IT'S A LEGIT DELIVERY JOB!
WHAT'S WRONG WITH GETTING PAID FOR THAT?!
lub dub
A JOB...
YOUR HEART AND SOUL ...
plip
OKAY, CENT!
DON'T BE SCARED OF THE FIRE! IT'LL HELP YOU DODGE THE BONE! YOU KNOW WHAT TO DO...
SWFF
ZIP

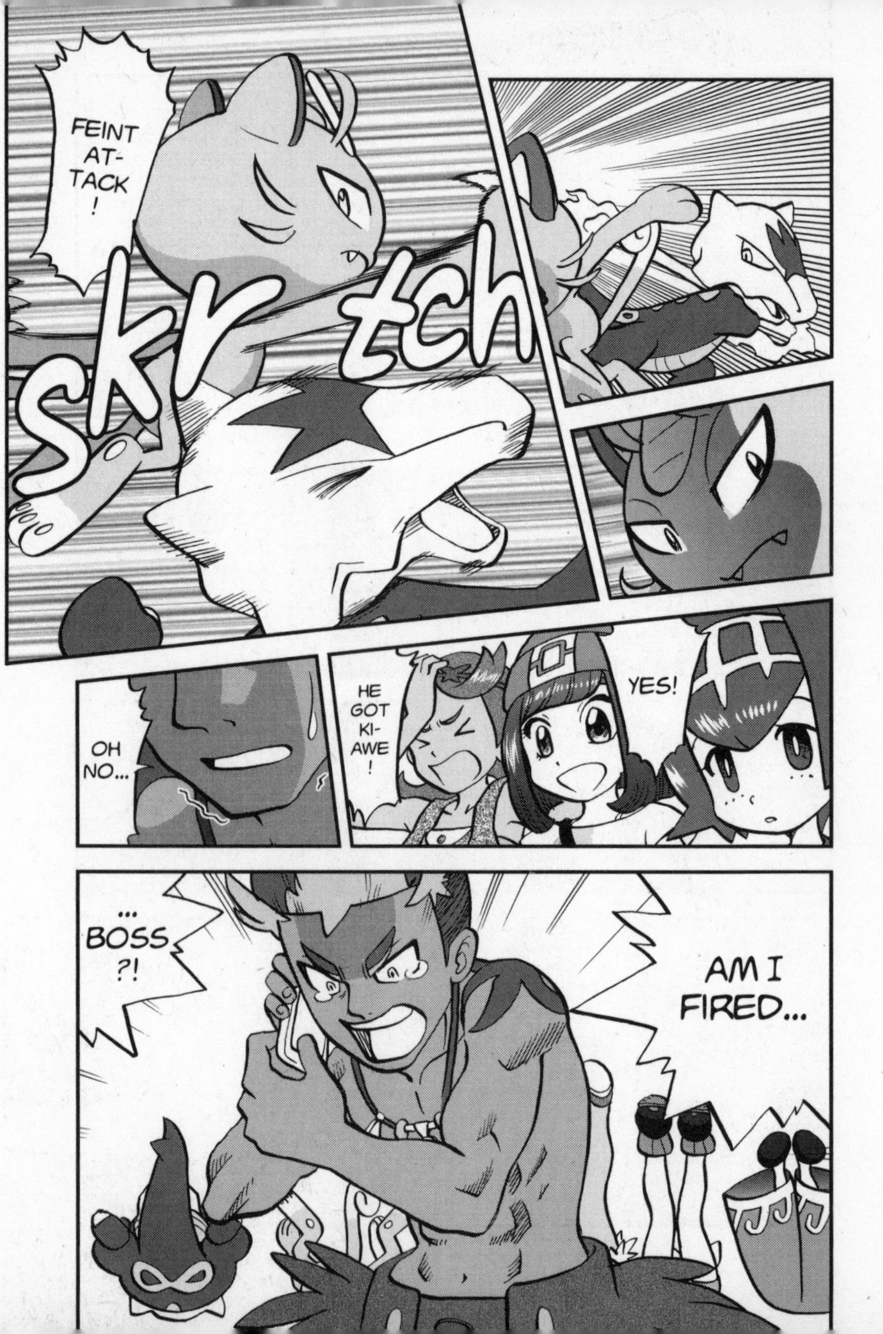
FEINT ATTACK!
SKR TCH
YES!
HE GOT KIAWE!
OH NO...
AM I FIRED...
...BOSS?!

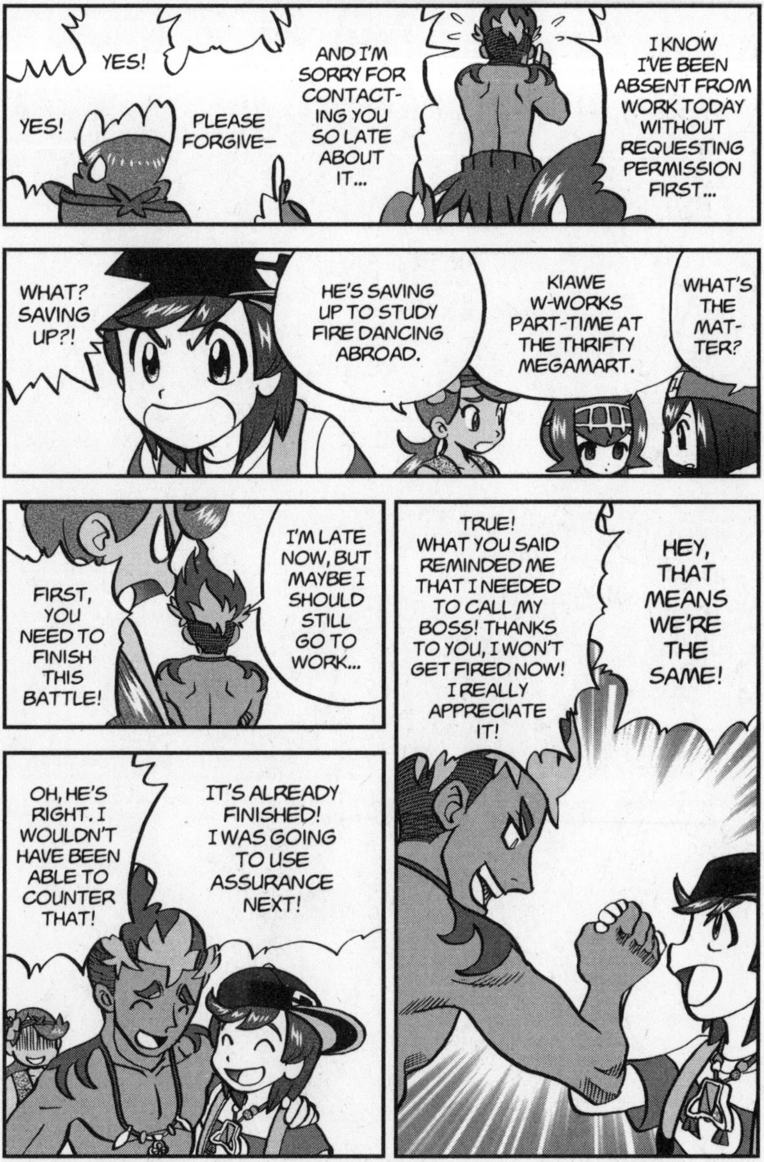
I KNOW I'VE BEEN ABSENT FROM WORK TODAY WITHOUT REQUESTING PERMISSION FIRST...
AND I'M SORRY FOR CONTACT-ING YOU SO LATE ABOUT IT...
PLEASE FORGIVE—
YES!
YES!
WHAT'S THE MAT-TER?
KIAWE W-WORKS PART-TIME AT THE THRIFTY MEGAMART.
HE'S SAVING UP TO STUDY FIRE DANCING ABROAD.
WHAT? SAVING UP?!
HEY, THAT MEANS WE'RE THE SAME!
TRUE! WHAT YOU SAID REMINDED ME THAT I NEEDED TO CALL MY BOSS! THANKS TO YOU, I WON'T GET FIRED NOW! I REALLY APPRECIATE IT!
I'M LATE NOW, BUT MAYBE I SHOULD STILL GO TO WORK...
FIRST, YOU NEED TO FINISH THIS BATTLE!
IT'S ALREADY FINISHED! I WAS GOING TO USE ASSURANCE NEXT!
OH, HE'S RIGHT. I WOULDN'T HAVE BEEN ABLE TO COUNTER THAT!

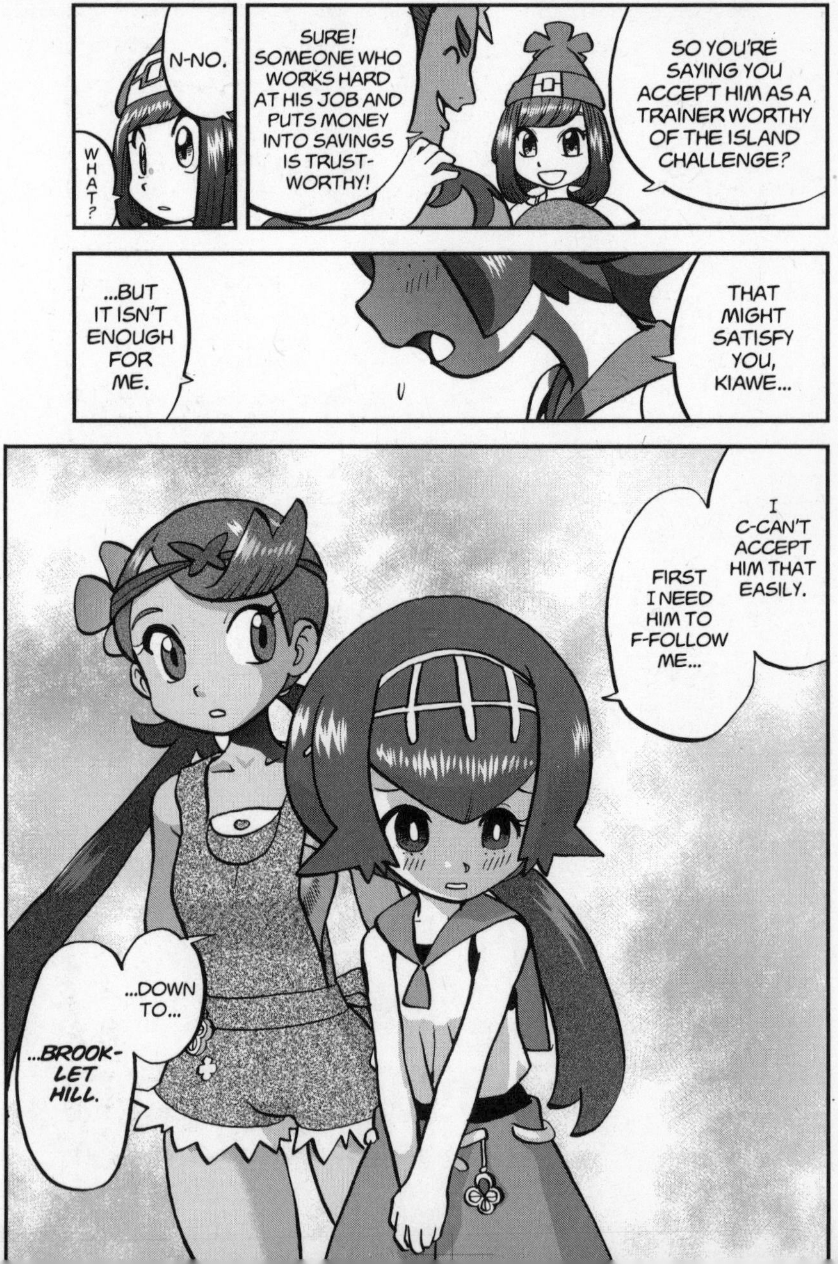
SO YOU'RE SAYING YOU ACCEPT HIM AS A TRAINER WORTHY OF THE ISLAND CHALLENGE?
SURE! SOMEONE WHO WORKS HARD AT HIS JOB AND PUTS MONEY INTO SAVINGS IS TRUST-WORTHY!
N-NO.
WHAT?
THAT MIGHT SATISFY YOU, KIAWE...
...BUT IT ISN'T ENOUGH FOR ME.
I C-CAN'T ACCEPT HIM THAT EASILY.
FIRST I NEED HIM TO F-FOLLOW ME...
...DOWN TO...
...BROOK-LET HILL.

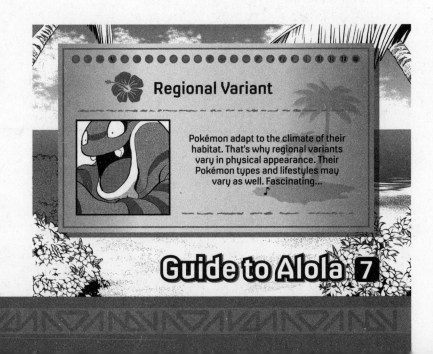

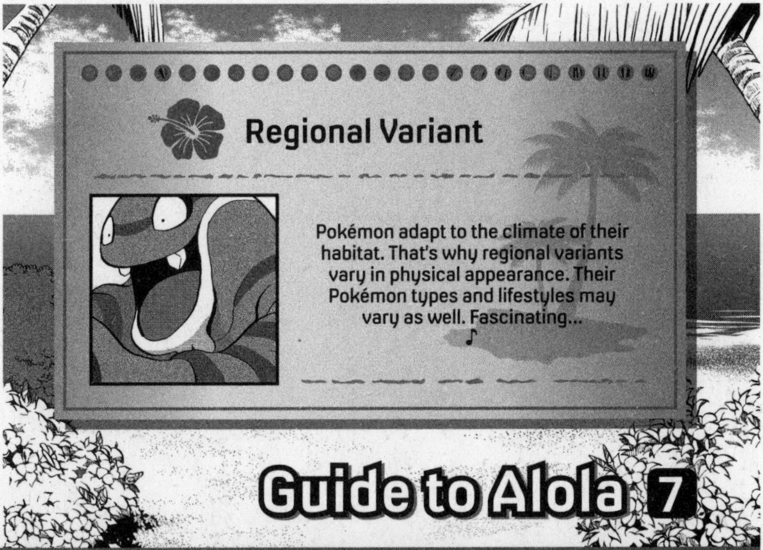
Regional Variant
Pokémon adapt to the climate of their habitat. That's why regional variants vary in physical appearance. Their Pokémon types and lifestyles may vary as well. Fascinating... ♪
Guide to Alola 7

Adventure 9
True Identity and the Totem Pokémon of Brooklet Hill

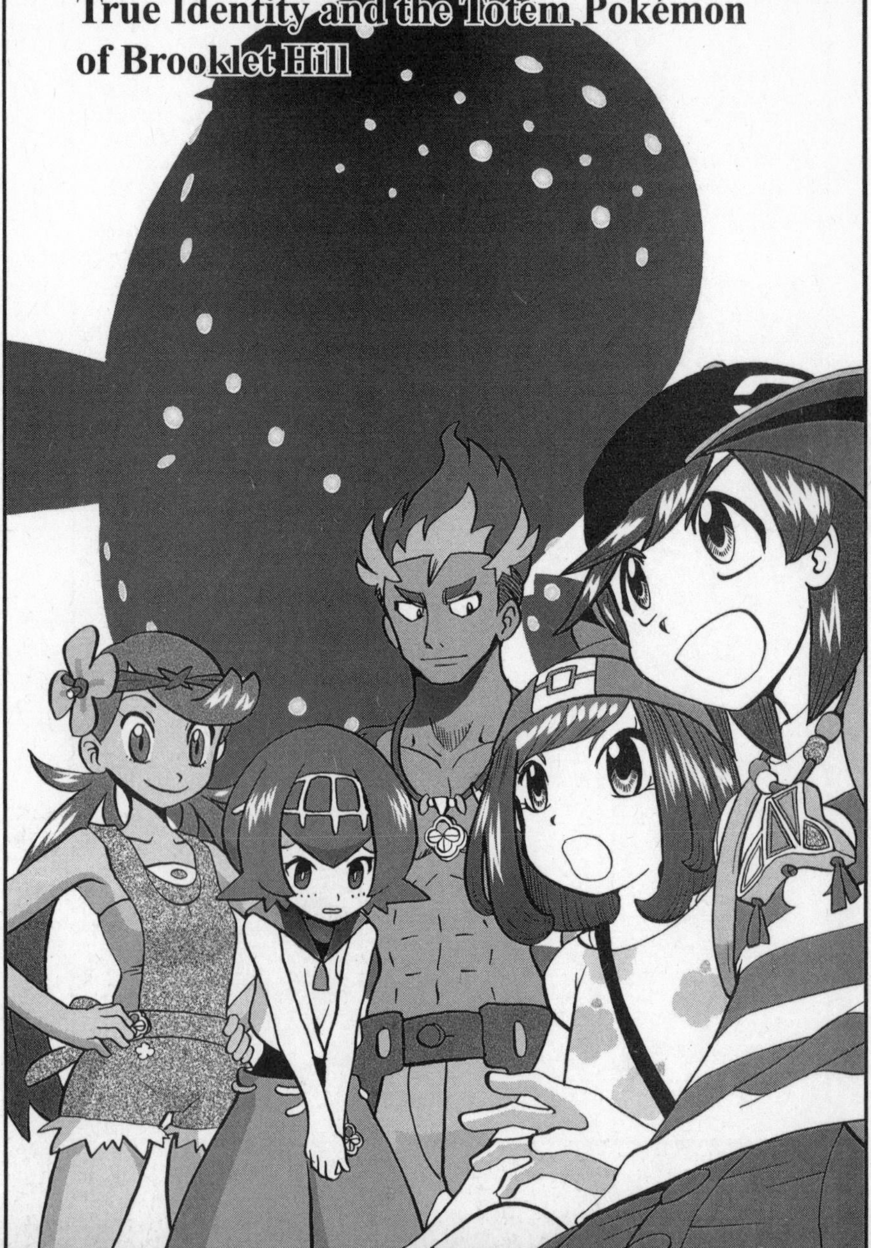

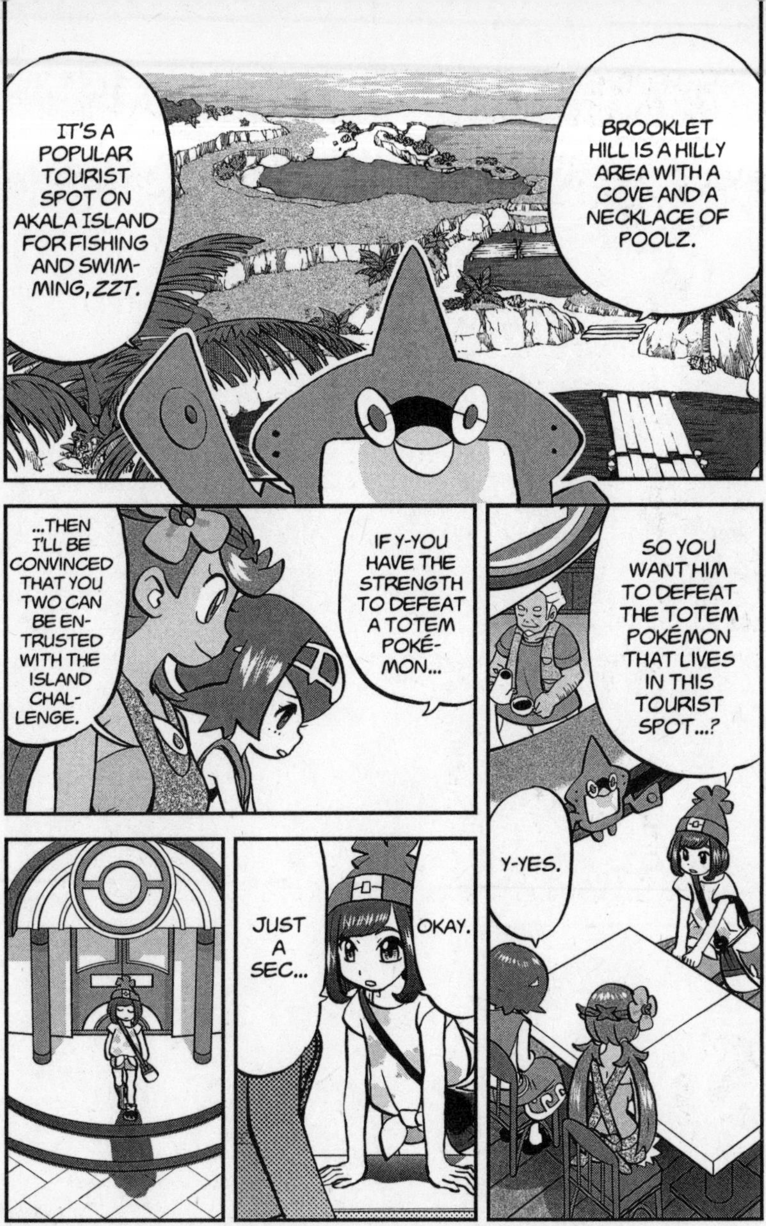
BROOKLET HILL IS A HILLY AREA WITH A COVE AND A NECKLACE OF POOLZ.
IT'S A POPULAR TOURIST SPOT ON AKALA ISLAND FOR FISHING AND SWIM-MING, ZZT.
SO YOU WANT HIM TO DEFEAT THE TOTEM POKÉMON THAT LIVES IN THIS TOURIST SPOT...?
Y-YES.
IF Y-YOU HAVE THE STRENGTH TO DEFEAT A TOTEM POKÉ-MON...
...THEN I'LL BE CONVINCED THAT YOU TWO CAN BE EN-TRUSTED WITH THE ISLAND CHAL-LENGE.
OKAY.
JUST A SEC...

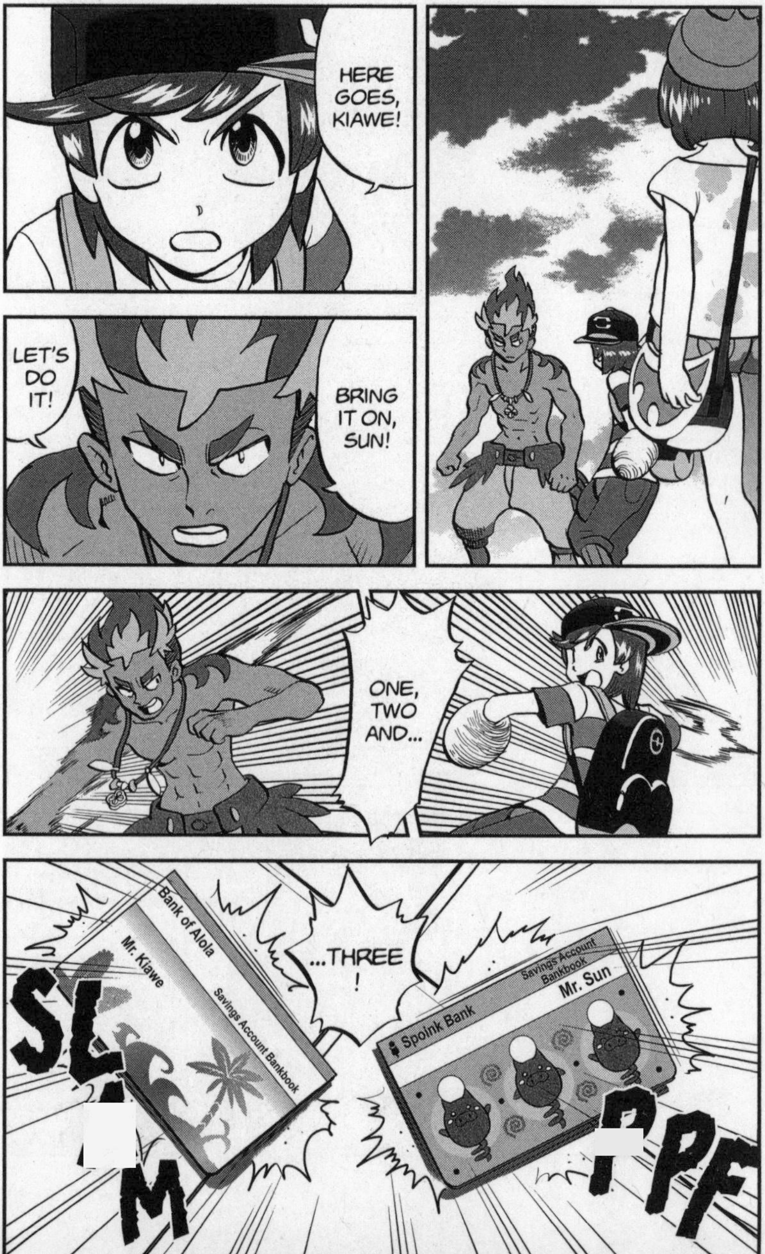
HERE GOES, KIAWE!
BRING IT ON, SUN!
LET'S DO IT!
ONE, TWO AND...
Savings Account Bankbook
Mr. Sun
Spoink Bank
...THREE!
Bank of Alola
Mr. Kiawe
Savings Account Bankbook

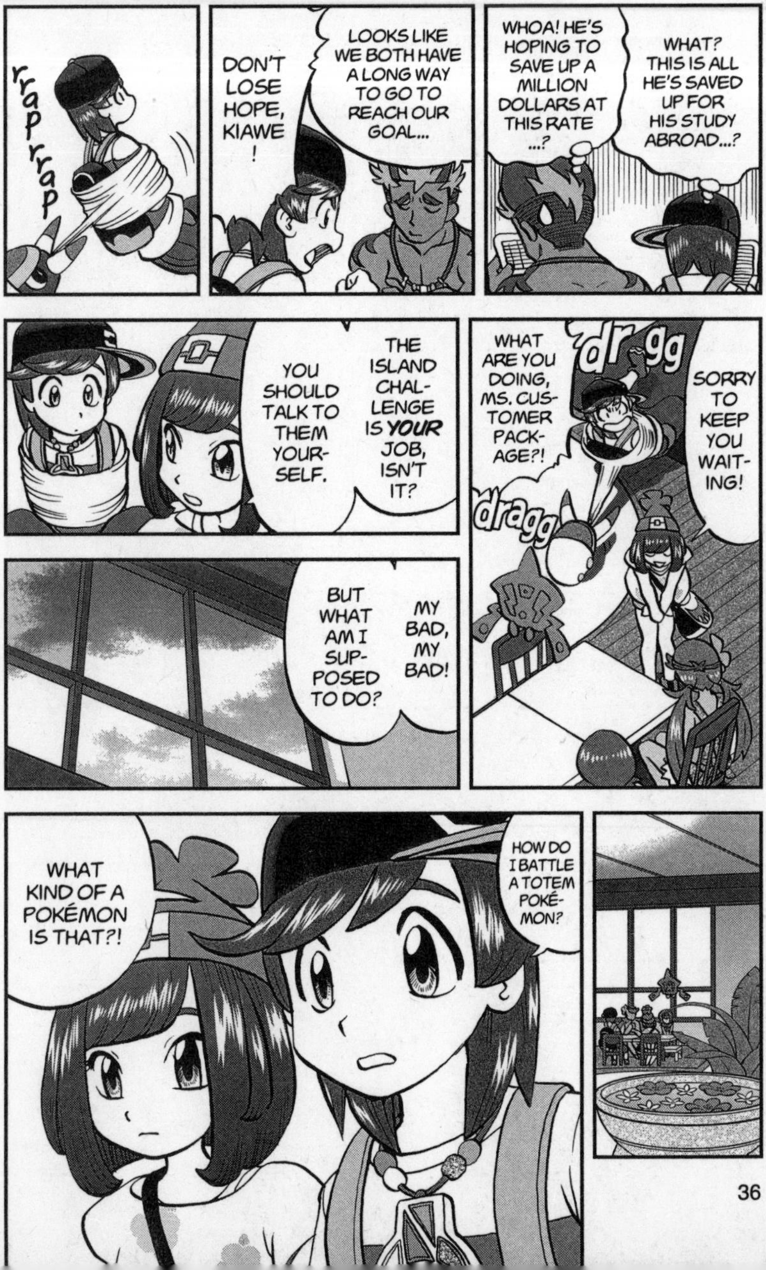
WHAT? THIS IS ALL HE'S SAVED UP FOR HIS STUDY ABROAD...?
WHOA! HE'S HOPING TO SAVE UP A MILLION DOLLARS AT THIS RATE ...?
LOOKS LIKE WE BOTH HAVE A LONG WAY TO GO TO REACH OUR GOAL...
DON'T LOSE HOPE, KIAWE!
rrap rrap rrap
dr-gg
SORRY TO KEEP YOU WAITING!
WHAT ARE YOU DOING, MS. CUSTOMER PACKAGE?!
dragg
THE ISLAND CHALLENGE IS **YOUR** JOB, ISN'T IT?
YOU SHOULD TALK TO THEM YOURSELF.
MY BAD, MY BAD!
BUT WHAT AM I SUPPOSED TO DO?
HOW DO I BATTLE A TOTEM POKÉMON?
WHAT KIND OF A POKÉMON IS THAT?!

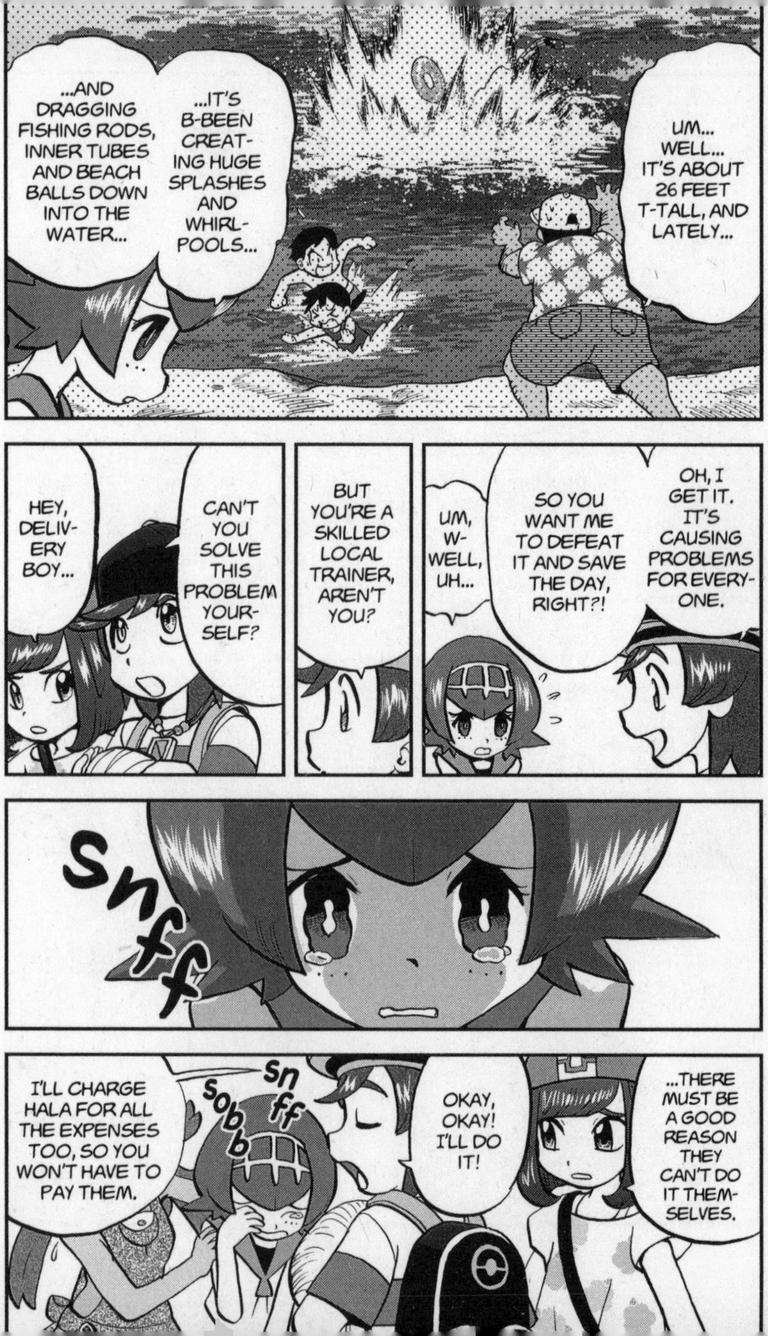
UM... WELL... IT'S ABOUT 26 FEET T-TALL, AND LATELY...
...IT'S B-BEEN CREAT-ING HUGE SPLASHES AND WHIRL-POOLS...
...AND DRAGGING FISHING RODS, INNER TUBES AND BEACH BALLS DOWN INTO THE WATER...
OH, I GET IT. IT'S CAUSING PROBLEMS FOR EVERY-ONE.
SO YOU WANT ME TO DEFEAT IT AND SAVE THE DAY, RIGHT?!
UM, W-WELL, UH...
BUT YOU'RE A SKILLED LOCAL TRAINER, AREN'T YOU?
CAN'T YOU SOLVE THIS PROBLEM YOUR-SELF?
HEY, DELIV-ERY BOY...
snff
...THERE MUST BE A GOOD REASON THEY CAN'T DO IT THEM-SELVES.
OKAY, OKAY! I'LL DO IT!
snff
sobb
I'LL CHARGE HALA FOR ALL THE EXPENSES TOO, SO YOU WON'T HAVE TO PAY THEM.

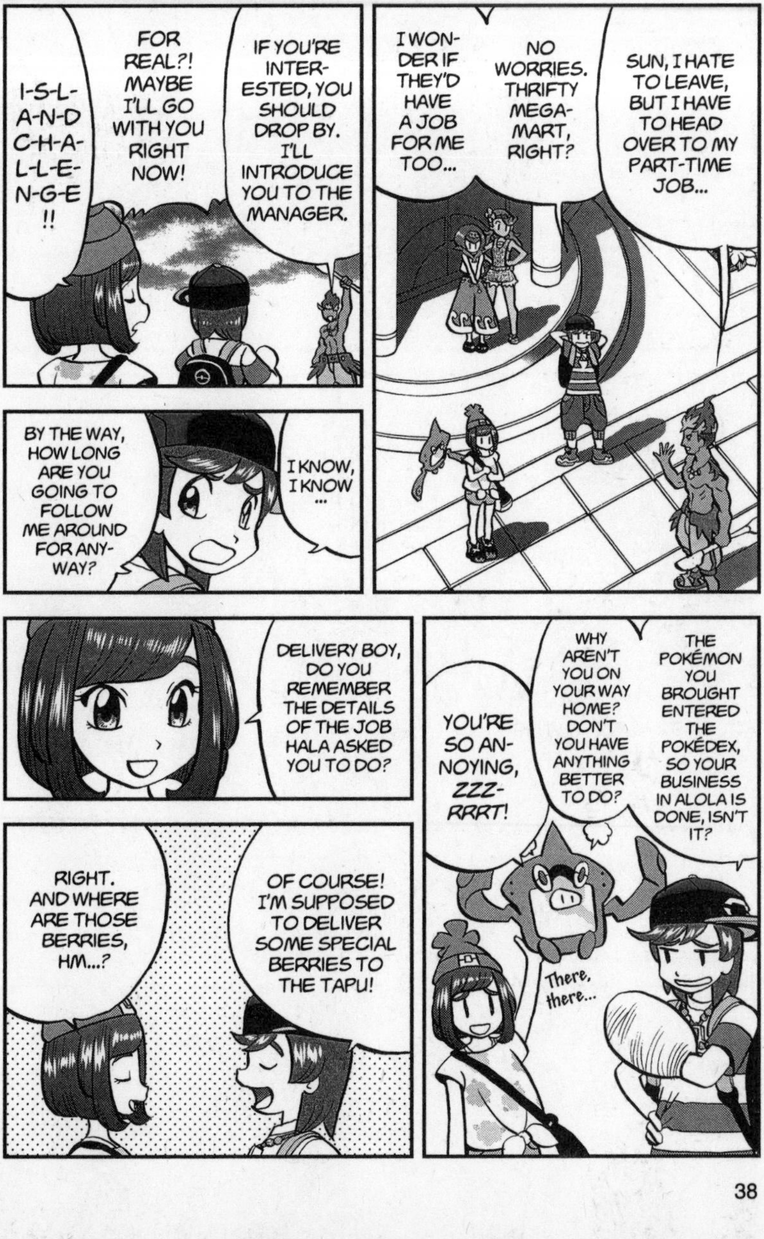
SUN, I HATE TO LEAVE, BUT I HAVE TO HEAD OVER TO MY PART-TIME JOB...
NO WORRIES. THRIFTY MEGA-MART, RIGHT?
I WON-DER IF THEY'D HAVE A JOB FOR ME TOO...
IF YOU'RE INTER-ESTED, YOU SHOULD DROP BY. I'LL INTRODUCE YOU TO THE MANAGER.
FOR REAL?! MAYBE I'LL GO WITH YOU RIGHT NOW!
I-S-L-A-N-D C-H-A-L-L-E-N-G-E !!
I KNOW, I KNOW ...
BY THE WAY, HOW LONG ARE YOU GOING TO FOLLOW ME AROUND FOR ANY-WAY?
THE POKÉMON YOU BROUGHT ENTERED THE POKÉDEX, SO YOUR BUSINESS IN ALOLA IS DONE, ISN'T IT?
WHY AREN'T YOU ON YOUR WAY HOME? DON'T YOU HAVE ANYTHING BETTER TO DO?
YOU'RE SO AN-NOYING, ZZZ-RRRT!
There, there...
DELIVERY BOY, DO YOU REMEMBER THE DETAILS OF THE JOB HALA ASKED YOU TO DO?
OF COURSE! I'M SUPPOSED TO DELIVER SOME SPECIAL BERRIES TO THE TAPU!
RIGHT. AND WHERE ARE THOSE BERRIES, HM...?

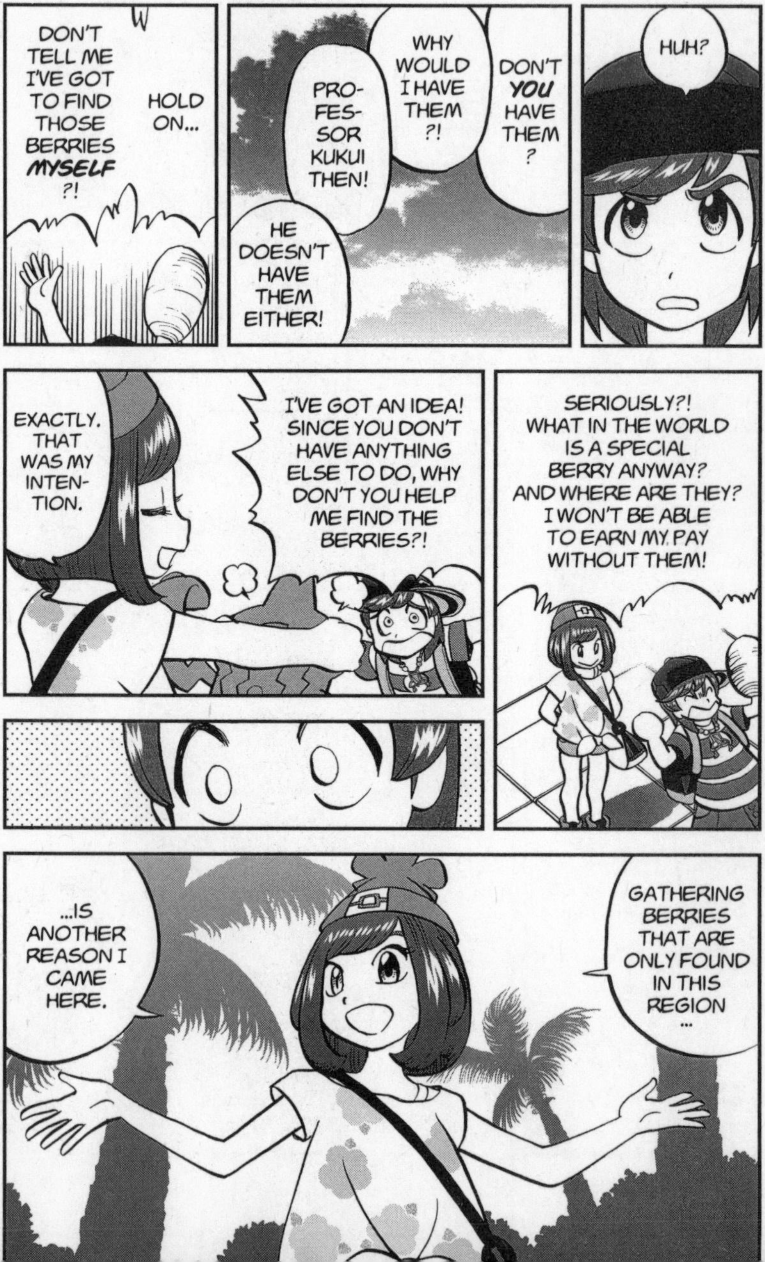
HUH?
DON'T YOU HAVE THEM?
WHY WOULD I HAVE THEM?!
PROFESSOR KUKUI THEN!
HE DOESN'T HAVE THEM EITHER!
HOLD ON...
DON'T TELL ME I'VE GOT TO FIND THOSE BERRIES MYSELF?!
SERIOUSLY?! WHAT IN THE WORLD IS A SPECIAL BERRY ANYWAY? AND WHERE ARE THEY? I WON'T BE ABLE TO EARN MY PAY WITHOUT THEM!
I'VE GOT AN IDEA! SINCE YOU DON'T HAVE ANYTHING ELSE TO DO, WHY DON'T YOU HELP ME FIND THE BERRIES?!
EXACTLY. THAT WAS MY INTENTION.
GATHERING BERRIES THAT ARE ONLY FOUND IN THIS REGION ...
...IS ANOTHER REASON I CAME HERE.

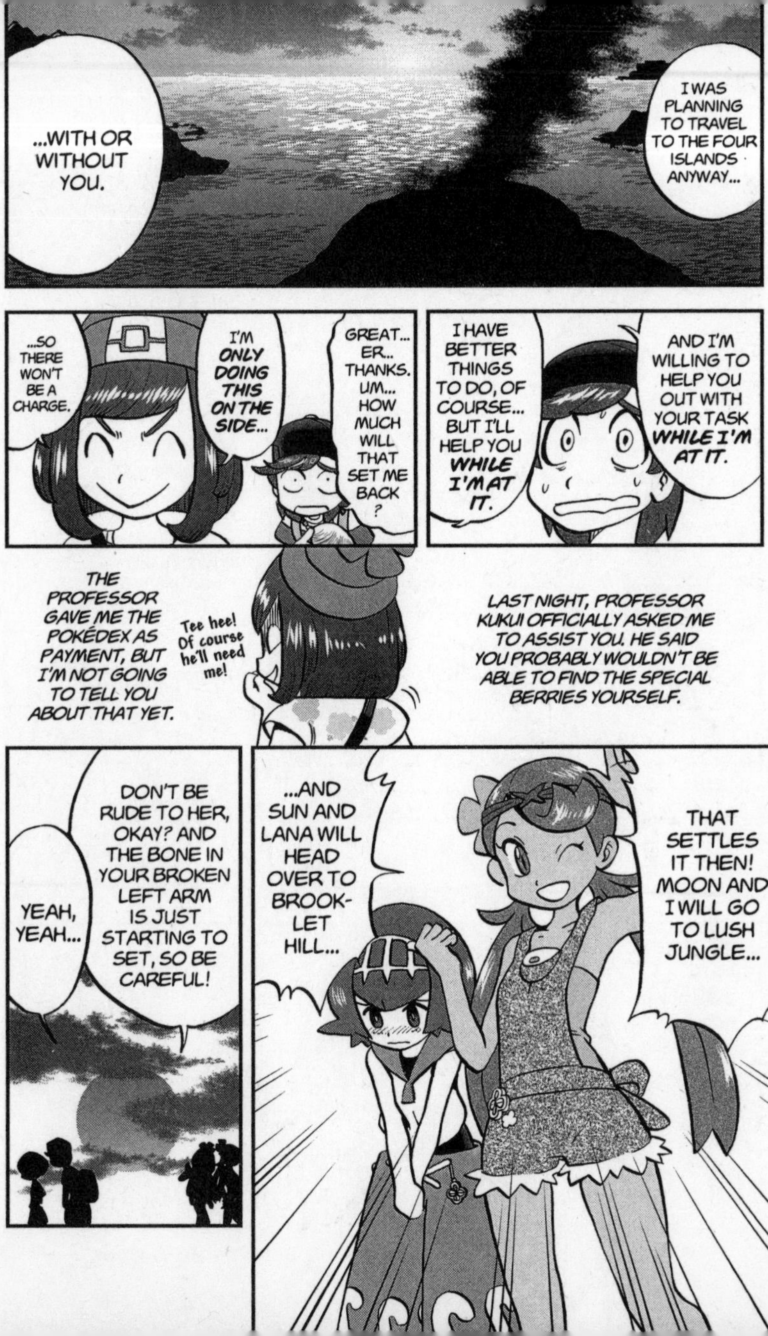
I WAS PLANNING TO TRAVEL TO THE FOUR ISLANDS ANYWAY...
...WITH OR WITHOUT YOU.
AND I'M WILLING TO HELP YOU OUT WITH YOUR TASK *WHILE I'M AT IT*.
I HAVE BETTER THINGS TO DO, OF COURSE... BUT I'LL HELP YOU *WHILE I'M AT IT*.
GREAT... ER.. THANKS. UM... HOW MUCH WILL THAT SET ME BACK?
I'M *ONLY DOING THIS ON THE SIDE*...
...SO THERE WON'T BE A CHARGE.
LAST NIGHT, PROFESSOR KUKUI OFFICIALLY ASKED ME TO ASSIST YOU. HE SAID YOU PROBABLY WOULDN'T BE ABLE TO FIND THE SPECIAL BERRIES YOURSELF.
Tee hee! Of course he'll need me!
THE PROFESSOR GAVE ME THE POKÉDEX AS PAYMENT, BUT I'M NOT GOING TO TELL YOU ABOUT THAT YET.
THAT SETTLES IT THEN! MOON AND I WILL GO TO LUSH JUNGLE...
...AND SUN AND LANA WILL HEAD OVER TO BROOK-LET HILL...
DON'T BE RUDE TO HER, OKAY? AND THE BONE IN YOUR BROKEN LEFT ARM IS JUST STARTING TO SET, SO BE CAREFUL!
YEAH, YEAH...

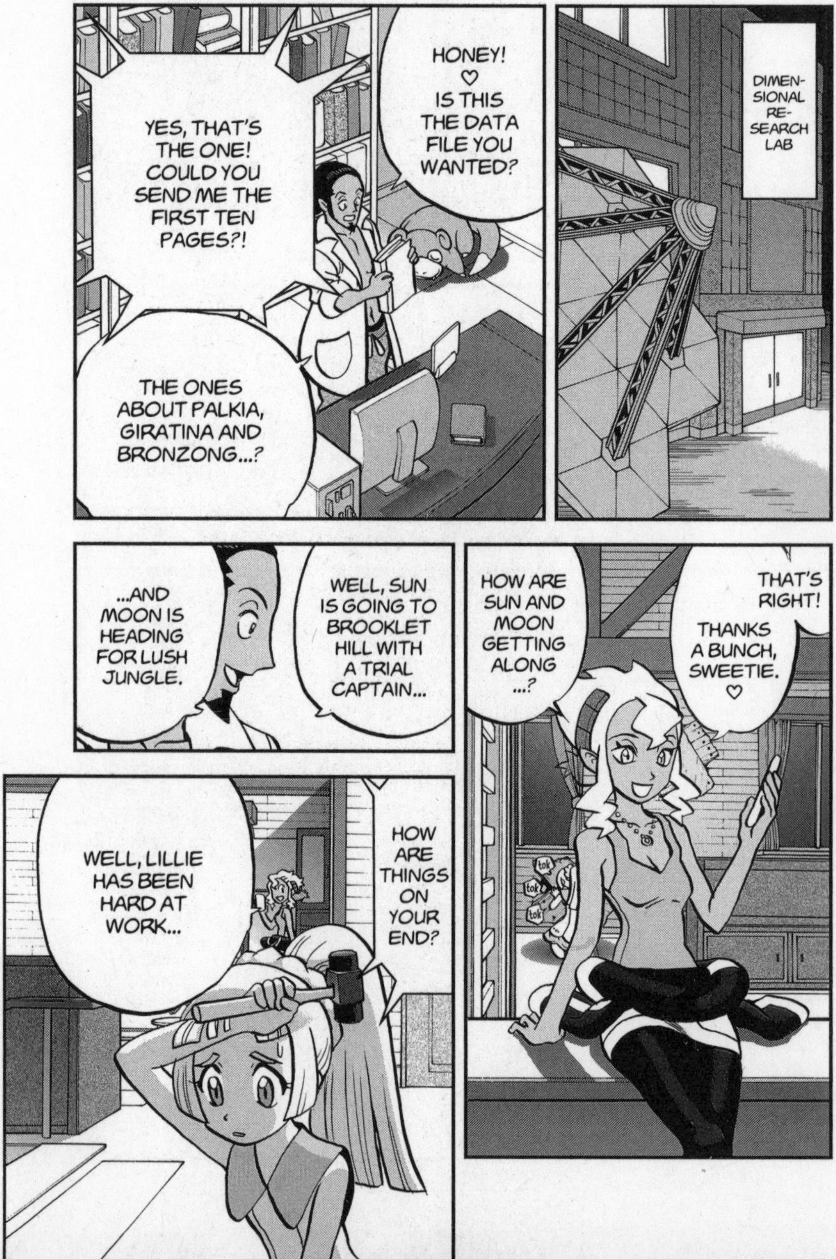
DIMEN-
SIONAL
RE-
SEARCH
LAB
HONEY! ♡ IS THIS THE DATA FILE YOU WANTED?
YES, THAT'S THE ONE! COULD YOU SEND ME THE FIRST TEN PAGES?!
THE ONES ABOUT PALKIA, GIRATINA AND BRONZONG...?
THAT'S RIGHT! THANKS A BUNCH, SWEETIE. ♡
HOW ARE SUN AND MOON GETTING ALONG ...?
tok
tok
tok
WELL, SUN IS GOING TO BROOKLET HILL WITH A TRIAL CAPTAIN...
...AND MOON IS HEADING FOR LUSH JUNGLE.
HOW ARE THINGS ON YOUR END?
WELL, LILLIE HAS BEEN HARD AT WORK...

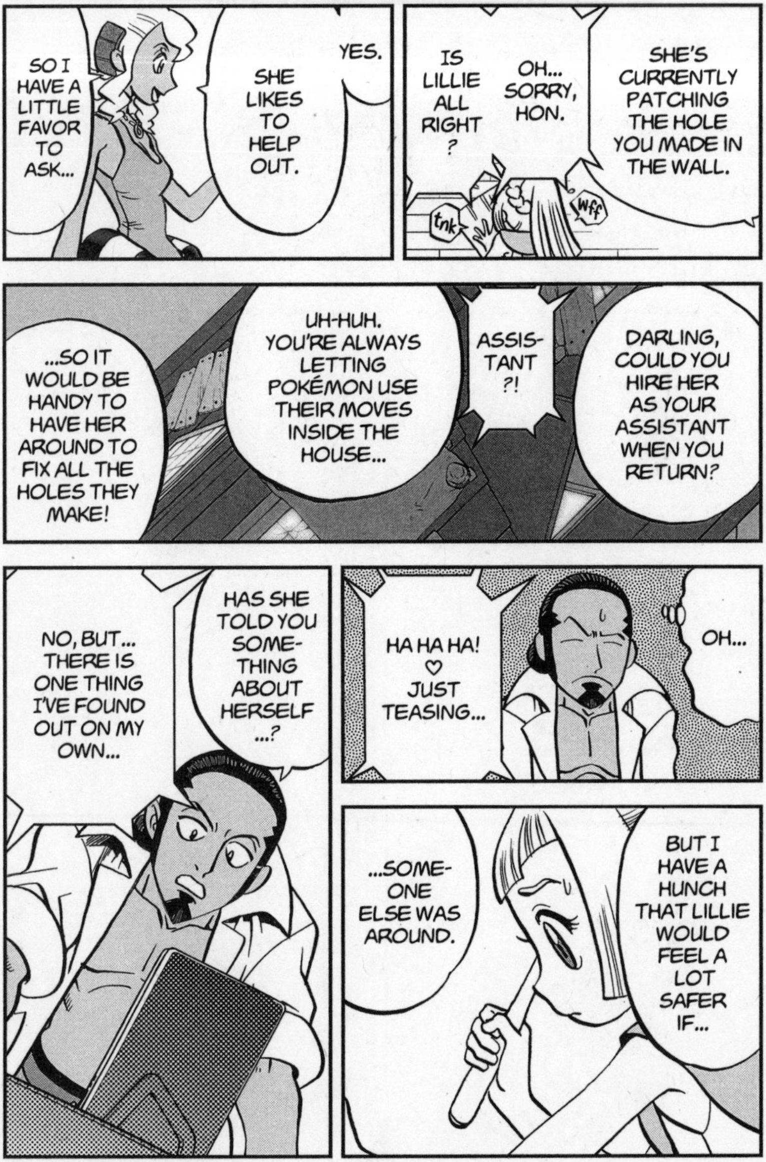
SHE'S CURRENTLY PATCHING THE HOLE YOU MADE IN THE WALL.
OH... SORRY, HON.
IS LILLIE ALL RIGHT?
wff
tnk
YES.
SHE LIKES TO HELP OUT.
SO I HAVE A LITTLE FAVOR TO ASK...
DARLING, COULD YOU HIRE HER AS YOUR ASSISTANT WHEN YOU RETURN?
ASSIS-TANT?!
UH-HUH. YOU'RE ALWAYS LETTING POKÉMON USE THEIR MOVES INSIDE THE HOUSE...
...SO IT WOULD BE HANDY TO HAVE HER AROUND TO FIX ALL THE HOLES THEY MAKE!
OH...
HA HA HA! ♡ JUST TEASING...
BUT I HAVE A HUNCH THAT LILLIE WOULD FEEL A LOT SAFER IF...
...SOME-ONE ELSE WAS AROUND.
HAS SHE TOLD YOU SOME-THING ABOUT HERSELF...?
NO, BUT... THERE IS ONE THING I'VE FOUND OUT ON MY OWN...

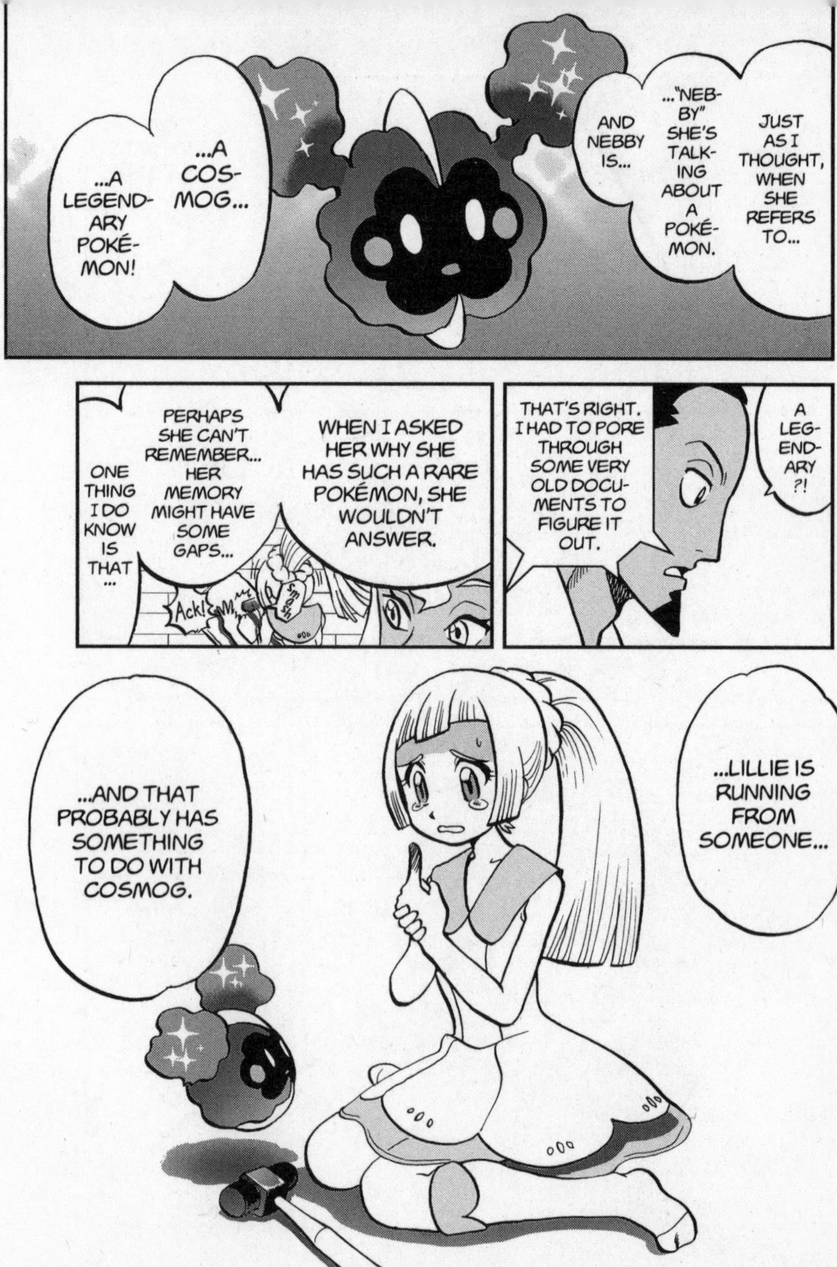
JUST AS I THOUGHT, WHEN SHE REFERS TO...
..."NEBBY" SHE'S TALKING ABOUT A POKÉMON.
AND NEBBY IS...
...A COSMOG...
...A LEGENDARY POKÉMON!
A LEGENDARY?!
THAT'S RIGHT. I HAD TO PORE THROUGH SOME VERY OLD DOCUMENTS TO FIGURE IT OUT.
WHEN I ASKED HER WHY SHE HAS SUCH A RARE POKÉMON, SHE WOULDN'T ANSWER.
PERHAPS SHE CAN'T REMEMBER... HER MEMORY MIGHT HAVE SOME GAPS...
Smash
Ack!
ONE THING I DO KNOW IS THAT...
...LILLIE IS RUNNING FROM SOMEONE...
...AND THAT PROBABLY HAS SOMETHING TO DO WITH COSMOG.

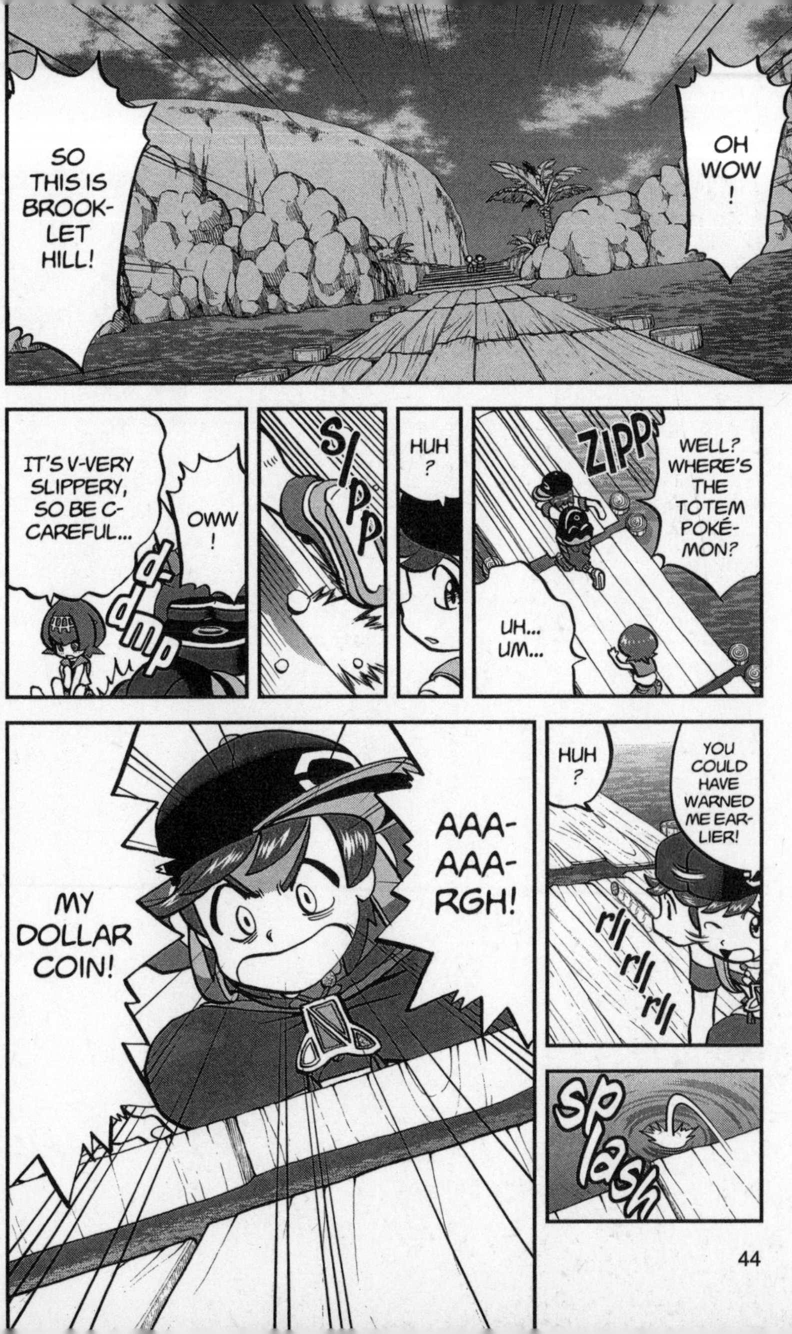
OH WOW !
SO THIS IS BROOK-LET HILL!
ZIPP
WELL? WHERE'S THE TOTEM POKÉ-MON?
UH... UM...
HUH ?
SlIPP
IT'S V-VERY SLIPPERY, SO BE C-CAREFUL...
OWW !
d-dmp
YOU COULD HAVE WARNED ME EAR-LIER!
HUH ?
rll rll rll rll
splash
AAA-AAAA-RGH!
MY DOLLAR COIN!

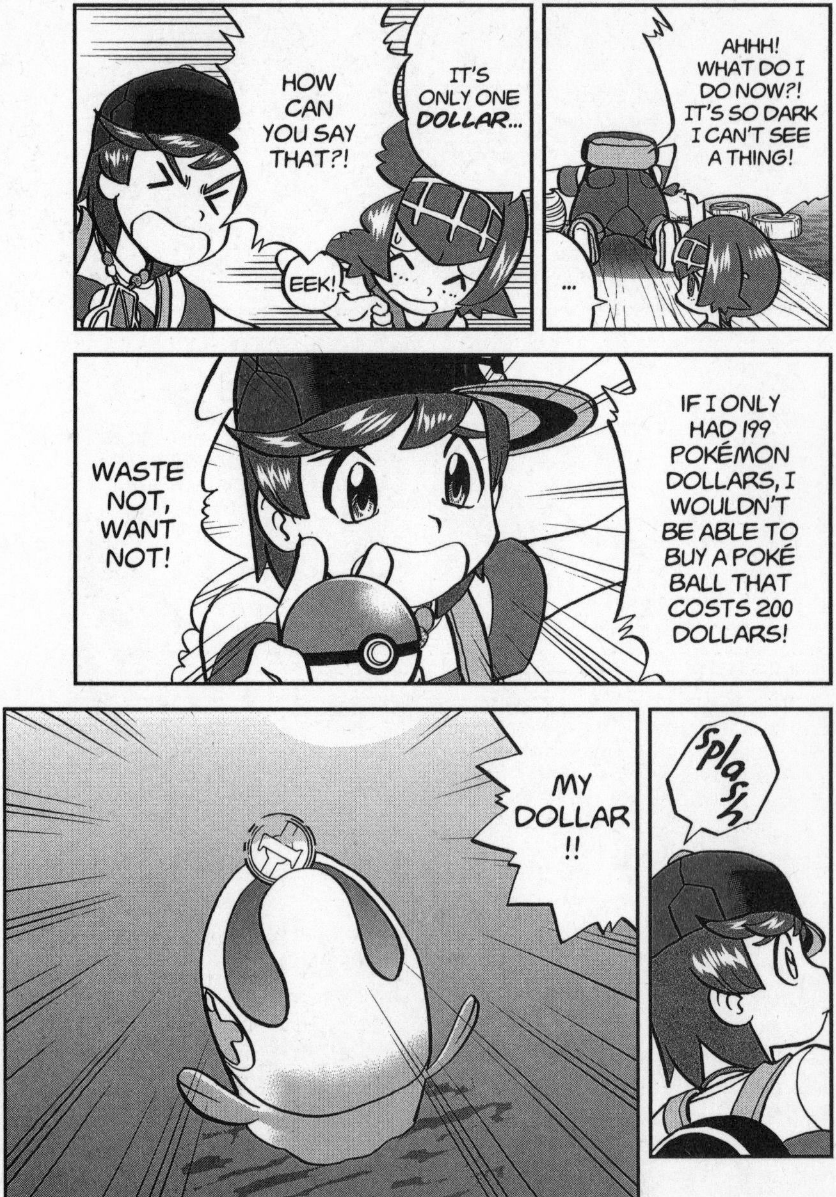
AHHH! WHAT DO I DO NOW?! IT'S SO DARK I CAN'T SEE A THING!
...
IT'S ONLY ONE **DOLLAR**...
HOW CAN YOU SAY THAT?!
EEK!
IF I ONLY HAD 199 POKÉMON DOLLARS, I WOULDN'T BE ABLE TO BUY A POKÉ BALL THAT COSTS 200 DOLLARS!
WASTE NOT, WANT NOT!
splash
MY DOLLAR !!

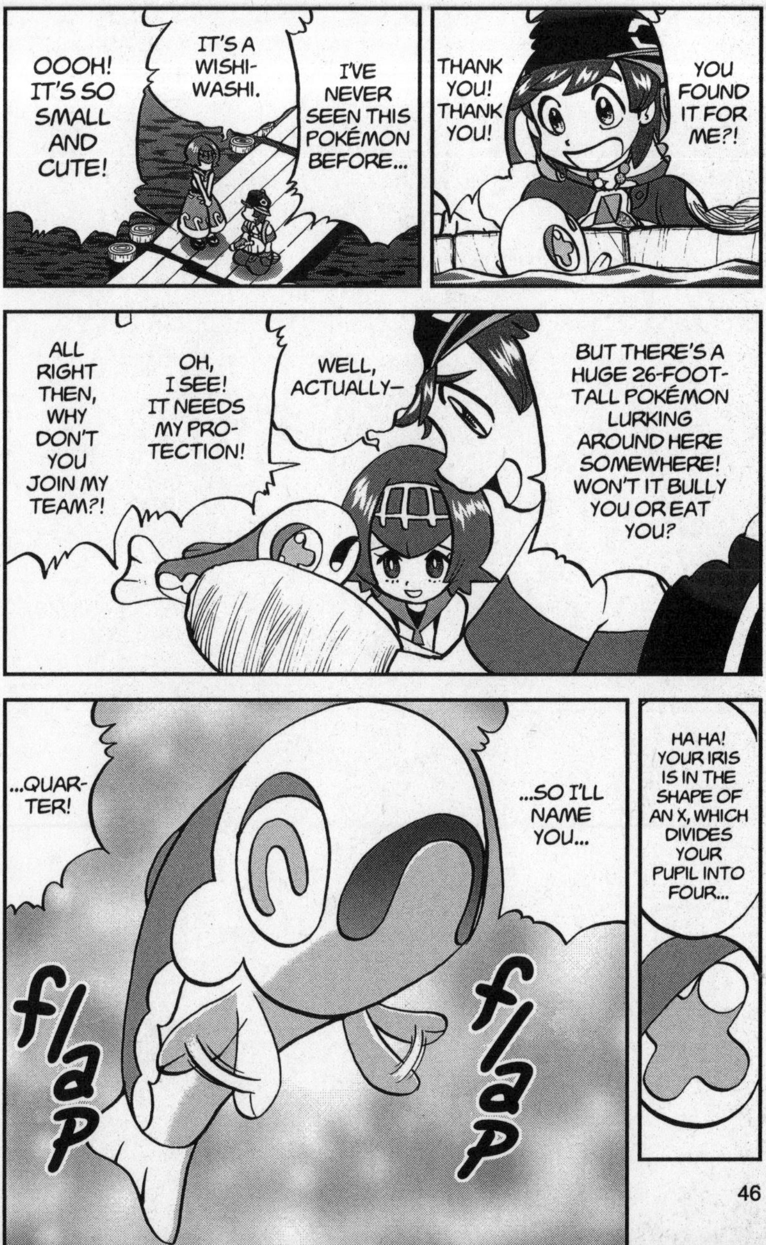
YOU FOUND IT FOR ME?!
THANK YOU! THANK YOU!
IT'S A WISHI-WASHI.
I'VE NEVER SEEN THIS POKÉMON BEFORE...
OOOH! IT'S SO SMALL AND CUTE!
BUT THERE'S A HUGE 26-FOOT-TALL POKÉMON LURKING AROUND HERE SOMEWHERE! WON'T IT BULLY YOU OR EAT YOU?
WELL, ACTUALLY—
OH, I SEE! IT NEEDS MY PRO-TECTION!
ALL RIGHT THEN, WHY DON'T YOU JOIN MY TEAM?!
HA HA! YOUR IRIS IS IN THE SHAPE OF AN X, WHICH DIVIDES YOUR PUPIL INTO FOUR...
...SO I'LL NAME YOU...
...QUARTER!
flap
flap

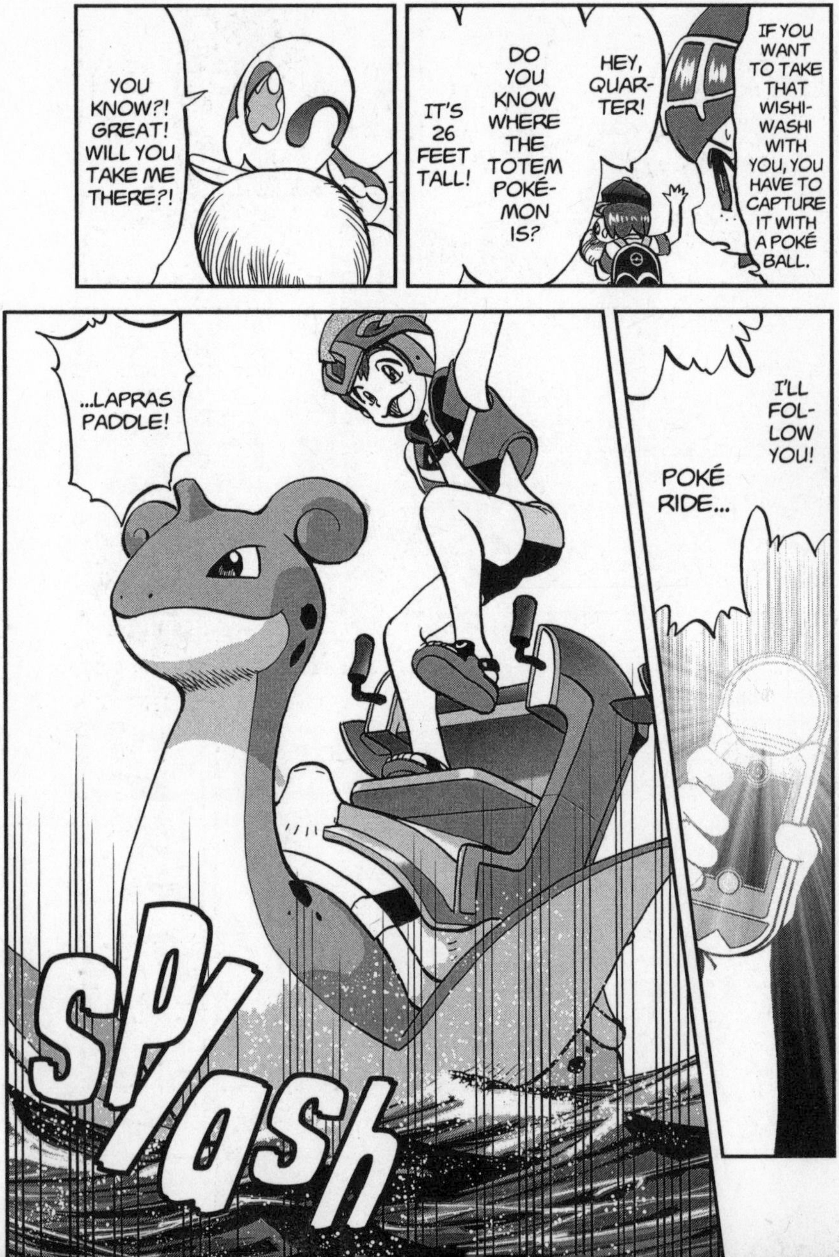
IF YOU WANT TO TAKE THAT WISHIWASHI WITH YOU, YOU HAVE TO CAPTURE IT WITH A POKÉ BALL.
HEY, QUARTER!
DO YOU KNOW WHERE THE TOTEM POKÉMON IS?
IT'S 26 FEET TALL!
YOU KNOW?! GREAT! WILL YOU TAKE ME THERE?!
I'LL FOLLOW YOU!
POKÉ RIDE...
...LAPRAS PADDLE!
SPLASH

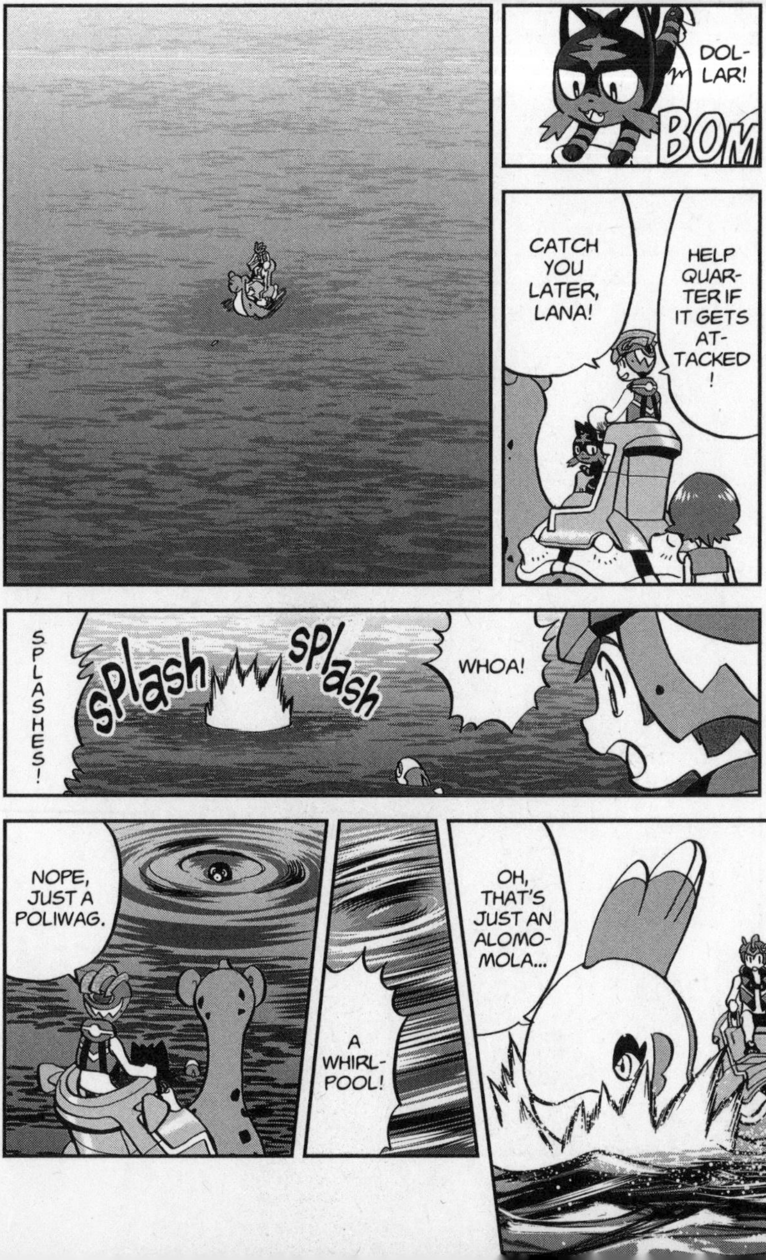
DOL-LAR!
BOM
HELP QUARTER IF IT GETS ATTACKED!
CATCH YOU LATER, LANA!
WHOA!
splash
splash
SPLASHES!
OH, THAT'S JUST AN ALOMOMOLA...
A WHIRLPOOL!
NOPE, JUST A POLIWAG.

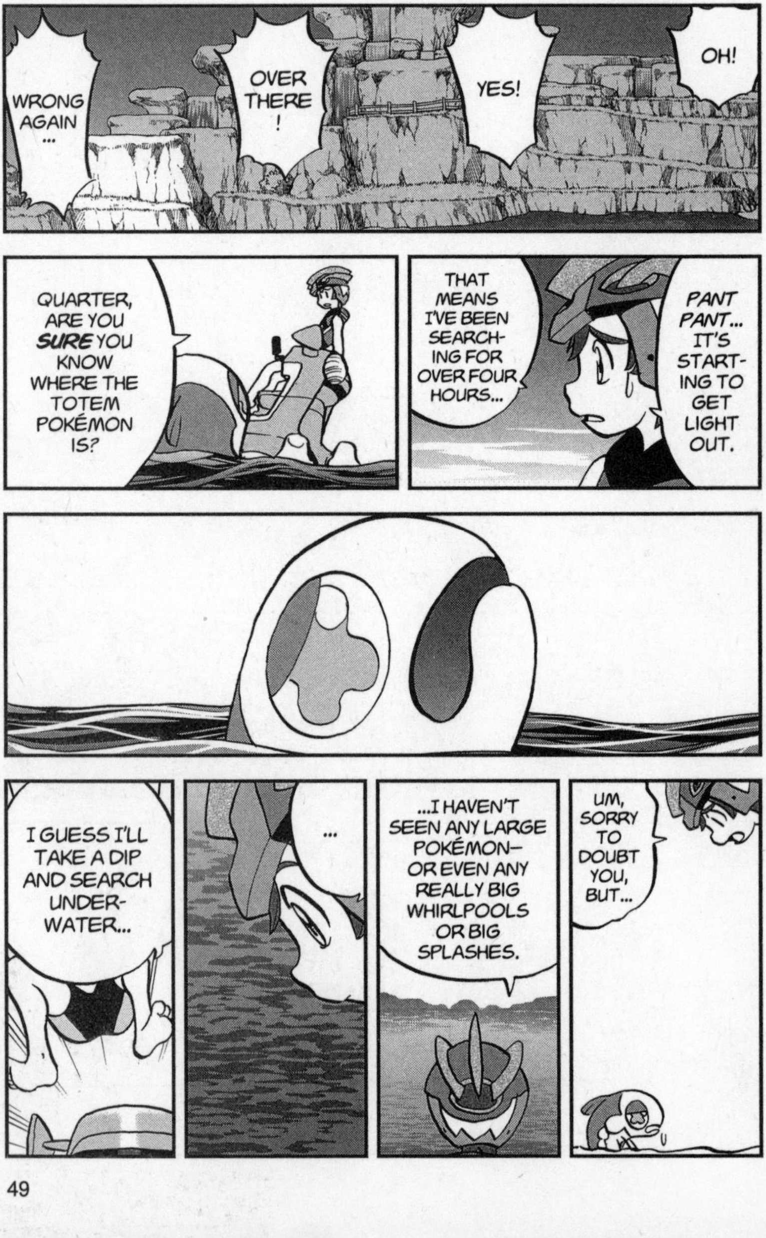
OH!
YES!
OVER THERE!
WRONG AGAIN...
PANT PANT... IT'S STARTING TO GET LIGHT OUT.
THAT MEANS I'VE BEEN SEARCHING FOR OVER FOUR HOURS...
QUARTER, ARE YOU SURE YOU KNOW WHERE THE TOTEM POKÉMON IS?
UM, SORRY TO DOUBT YOU, BUT...
...I HAVEN'T SEEN ANY LARGE POKÉMON—OR EVEN ANY REALLY BIG WHIRLPOOLS OR BIG SPLASHES.
...
I GUESS I'LL TAKE A DIP AND SEARCH UNDERWATER...

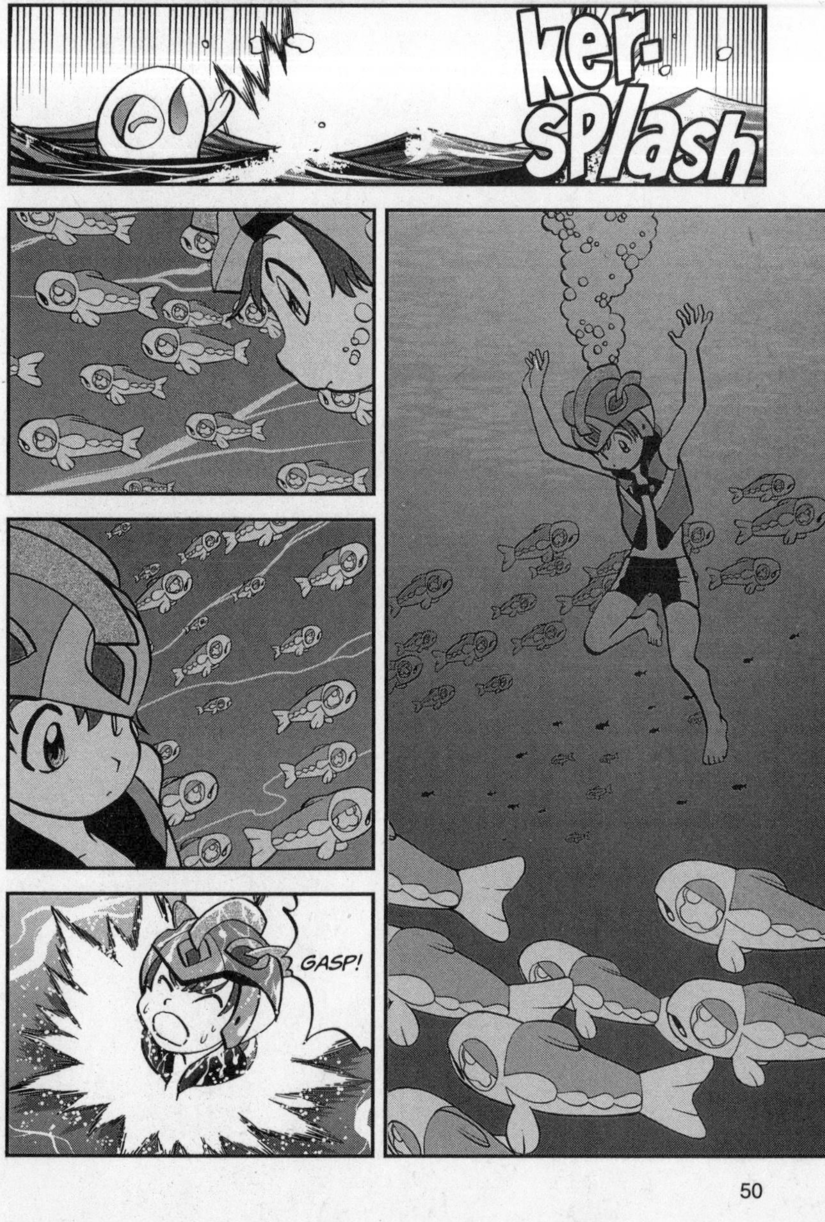
KER-SPLASH
GASP!

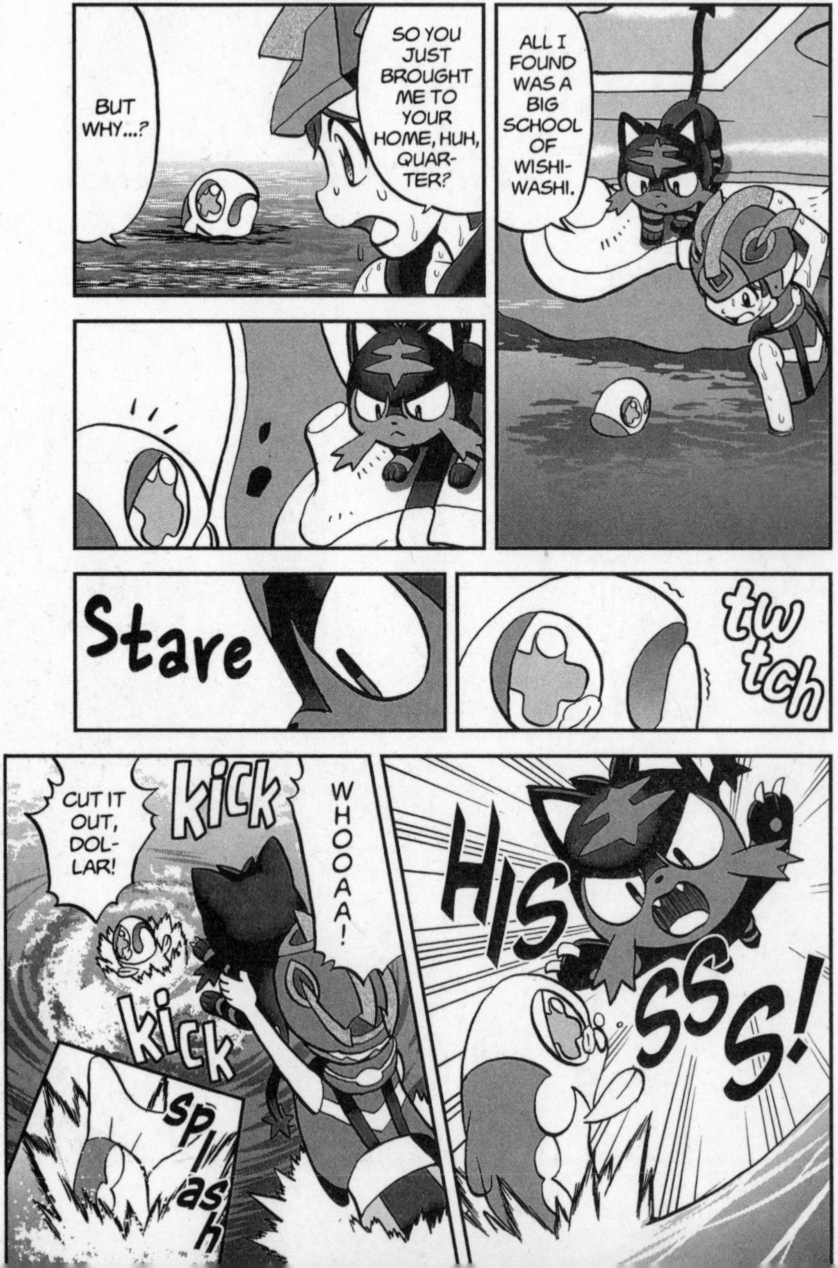
ALL I FOUND WAS A BIG SCHOOL OF WISHI-WASHI.
SO YOU JUST BROUGHT ME TO YOUR HOME, HUH, QUARTER?
BUT WHY...?
twtch
Stare
HISSSSS!
WHOOOAA!
kick
CUT IT OUT, DOL-LAR!
kick
splash

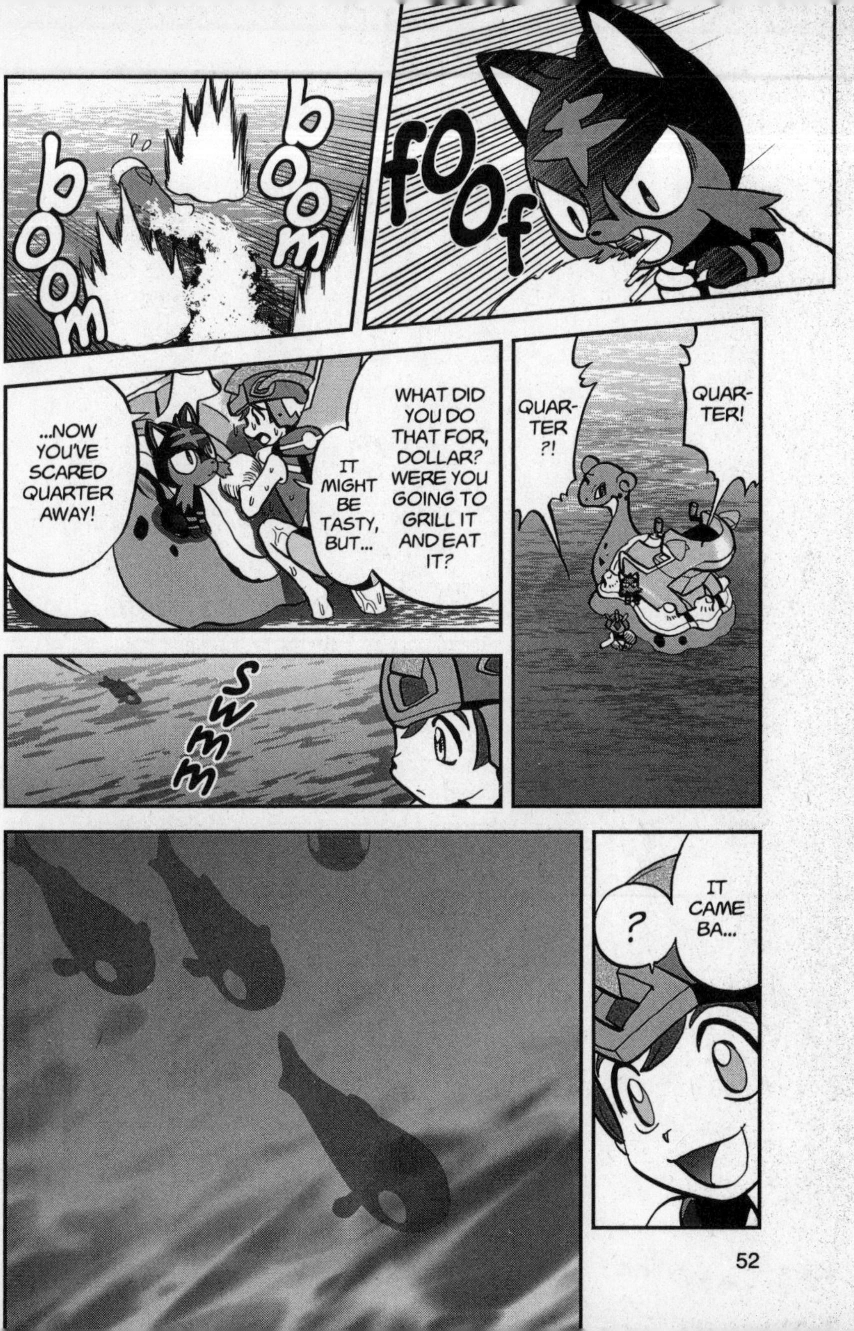
fOOf
boom
boom
QUARTER!
QUARTER?!
WHAT DID YOU DO THAT FOR, DOLLAR? WERE YOU GOING TO GRILL IT AND EAT IT?
IT MIGHT BE TASTY, BUT...
...NOW YOU'VE SCARED QUARTER AWAY!
swmm
IT CAME BA...
?
IT CAME BA...

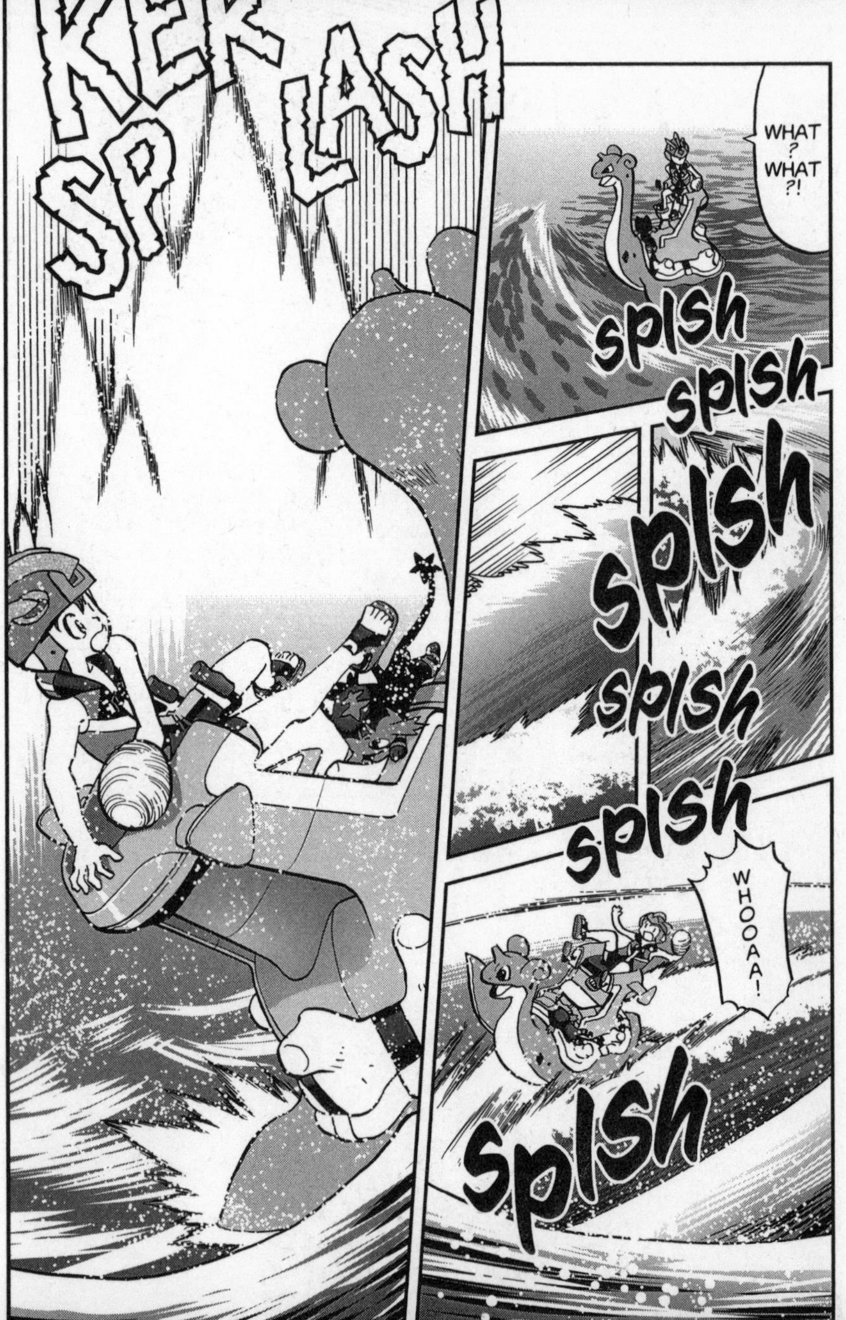
WHAT? WHAT?!
spish
spish
spish
spish
spish
WHOOAA!
spish
KER SPLASH

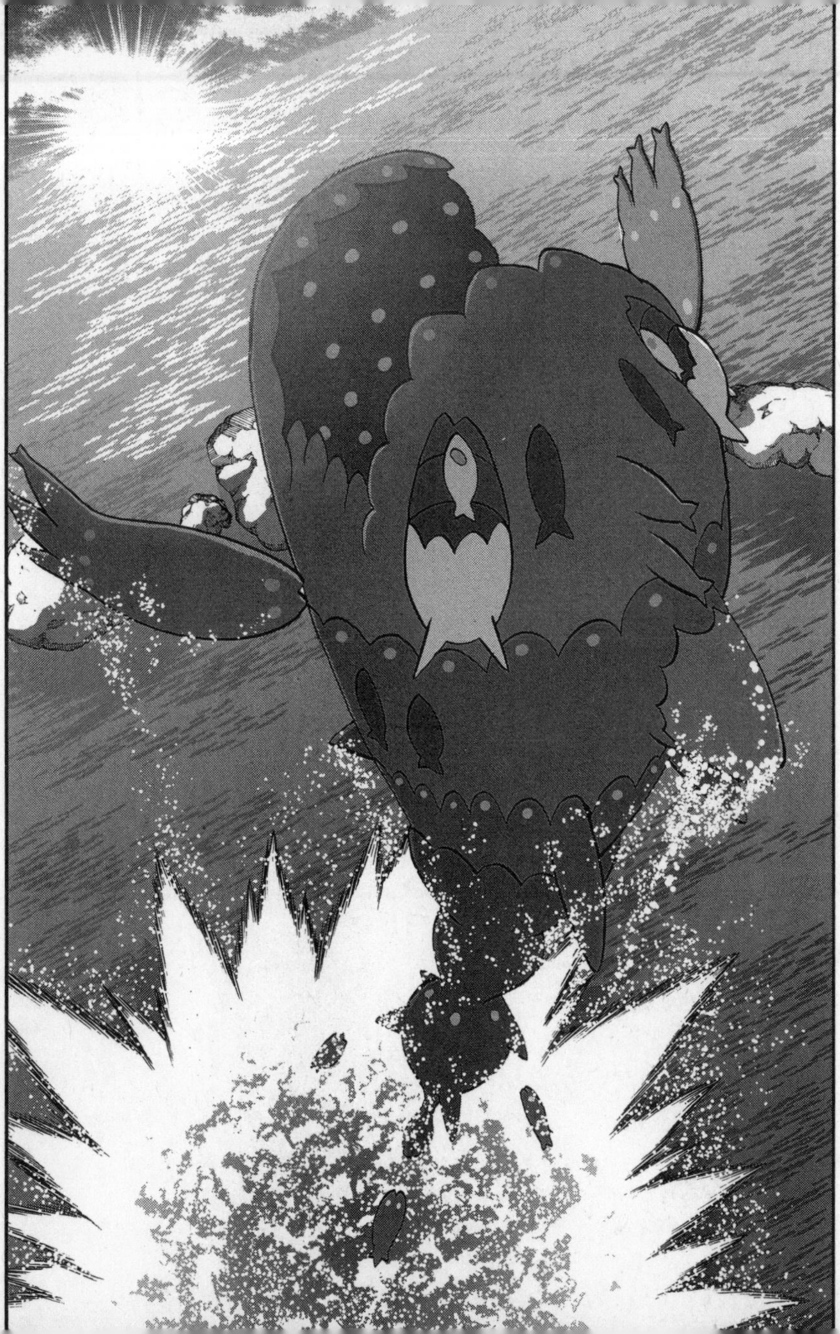

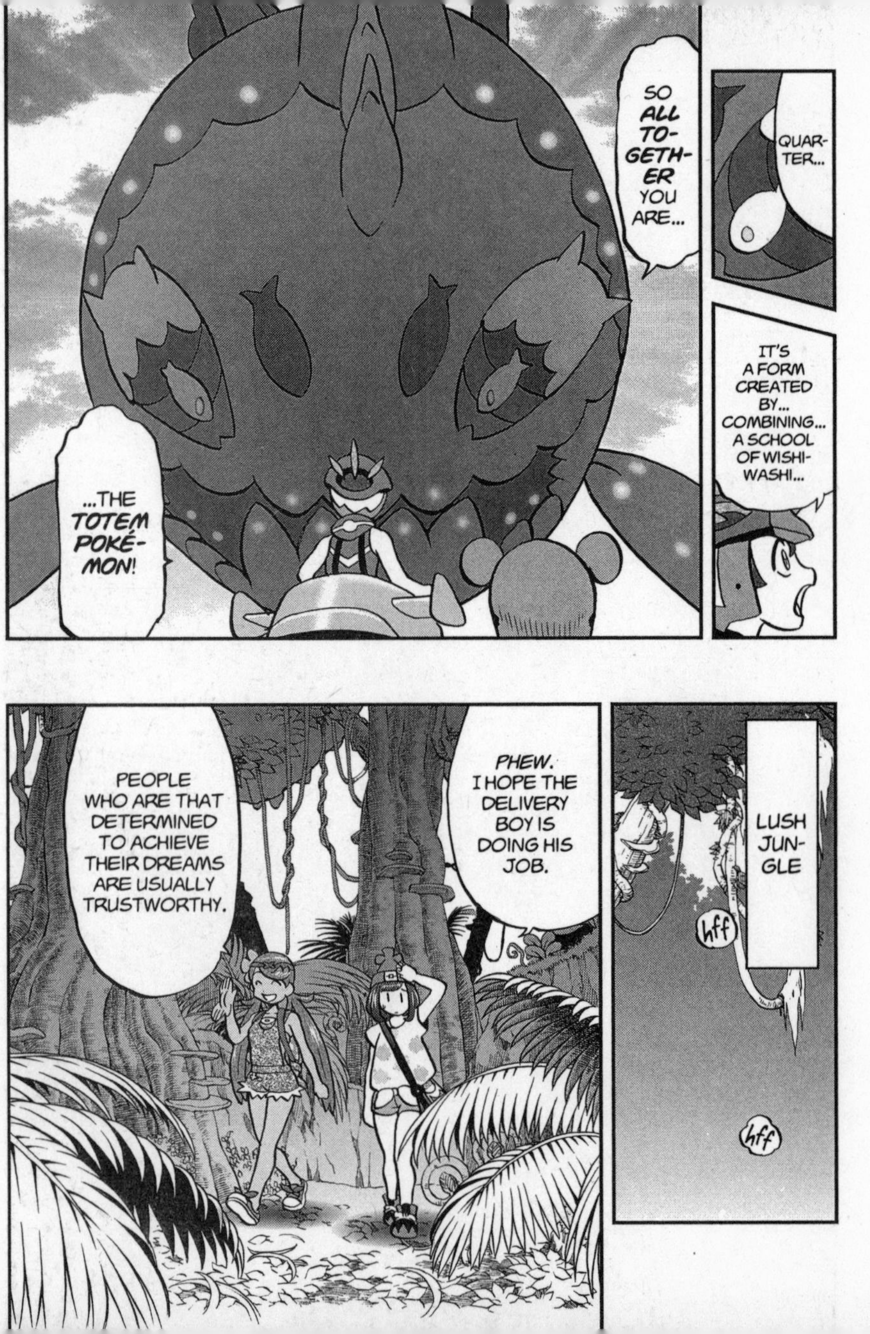
QUARTER...
IT'S A FORM CREATED BY... COMBINING... A SCHOOL OF WISHIWASHI...
SO **ALL TOGETHER** YOU ARE...
...THE *TOTEM POKÉMON*!
LUSH JUNGLE
hff
hff
PHEW. I HOPE THE DELIVERY BOY IS DOING HIS JOB.
PEOPLE WHO ARE THAT DETERMINED TO ACHIEVE THEIR DREAMS ARE USUALLY TRUSTWORTHY.

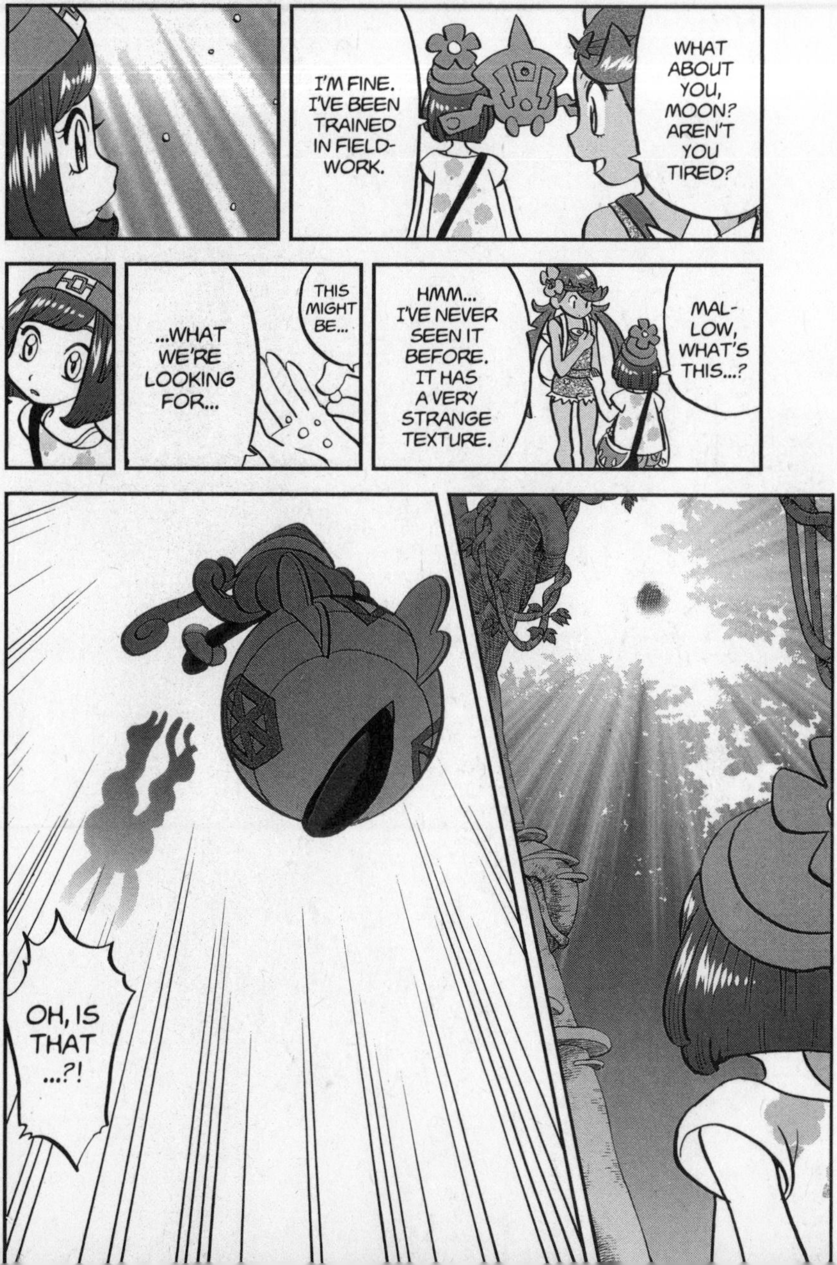
WHAT ABOUT YOU, MOON? AREN'T YOU TIRED?
I'M FINE. I'VE BEEN TRAINED IN FIELD-WORK.
MAL-LOW, WHAT'S THIS...?
HMM... I'VE NEVER SEEN IT BEFORE. IT HAS A VERY STRANGE TEXTURE.
THIS MIGHT BE...
...WHAT WE'RE LOOKING FOR...
OH, IS THAT ...?!

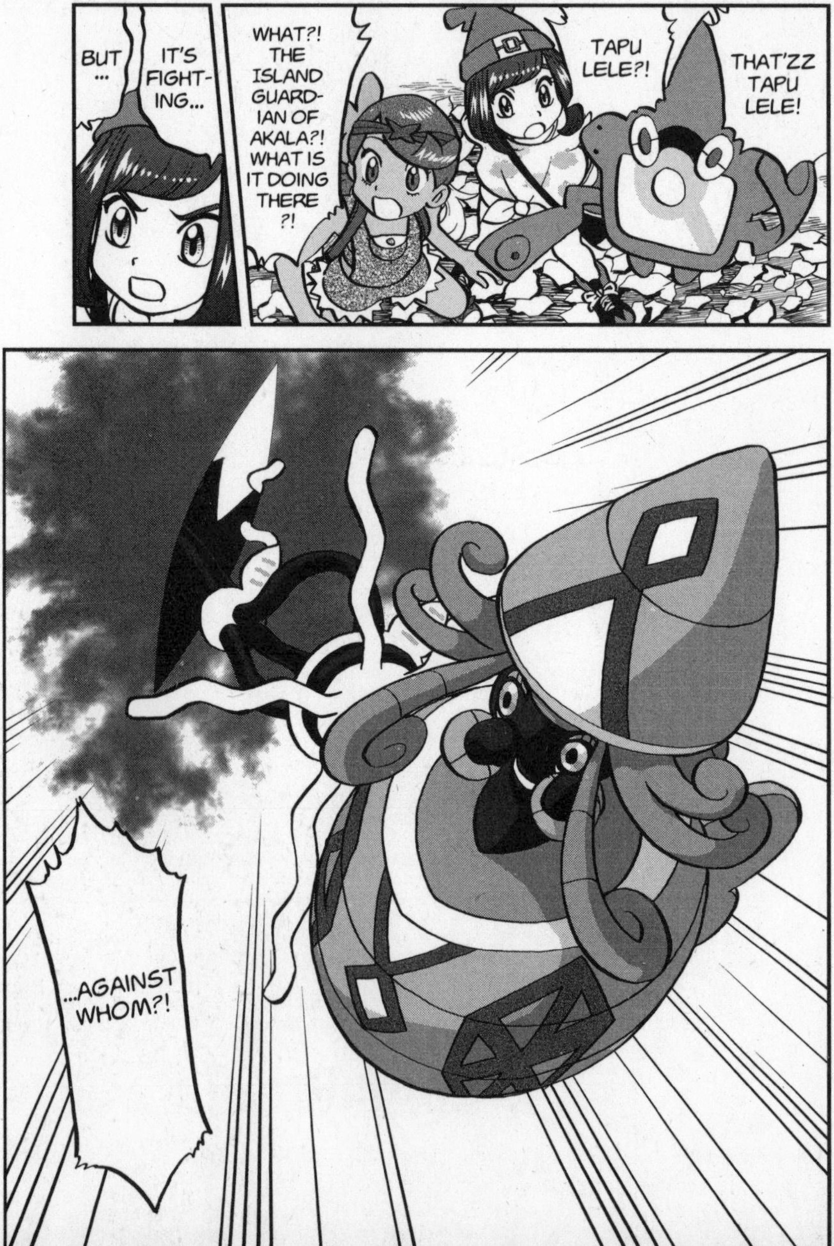
THAT'ZZ TAPU LELE!
TAPU LELE?!
WHAT?! THE ISLAND GUARDIAN OF AKALA?! WHAT IS IT DOING THERE?!
IT'S FIGHTING...
BUT...
...AGAINST WHOM?!

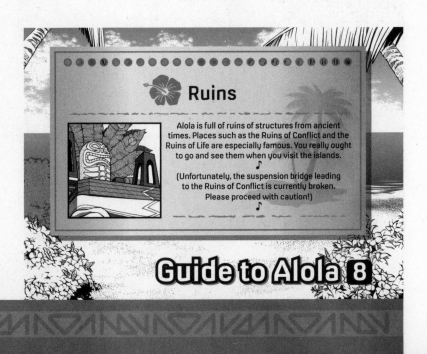

Ruins

Alola is full of ruins of structures from ancient times. Places such as the Ruins of Conflict and the Ruins of Life are especially famous. You really ought to go and see them when you visit the islands.

♪

(Unfortunately, the suspension bridge leading to the Ruins of Conflict is currently broken. Please proceed with caution!)

♪

Guide to Alola 8

Adventure 10
Defeat and the Commander of the School of Fish

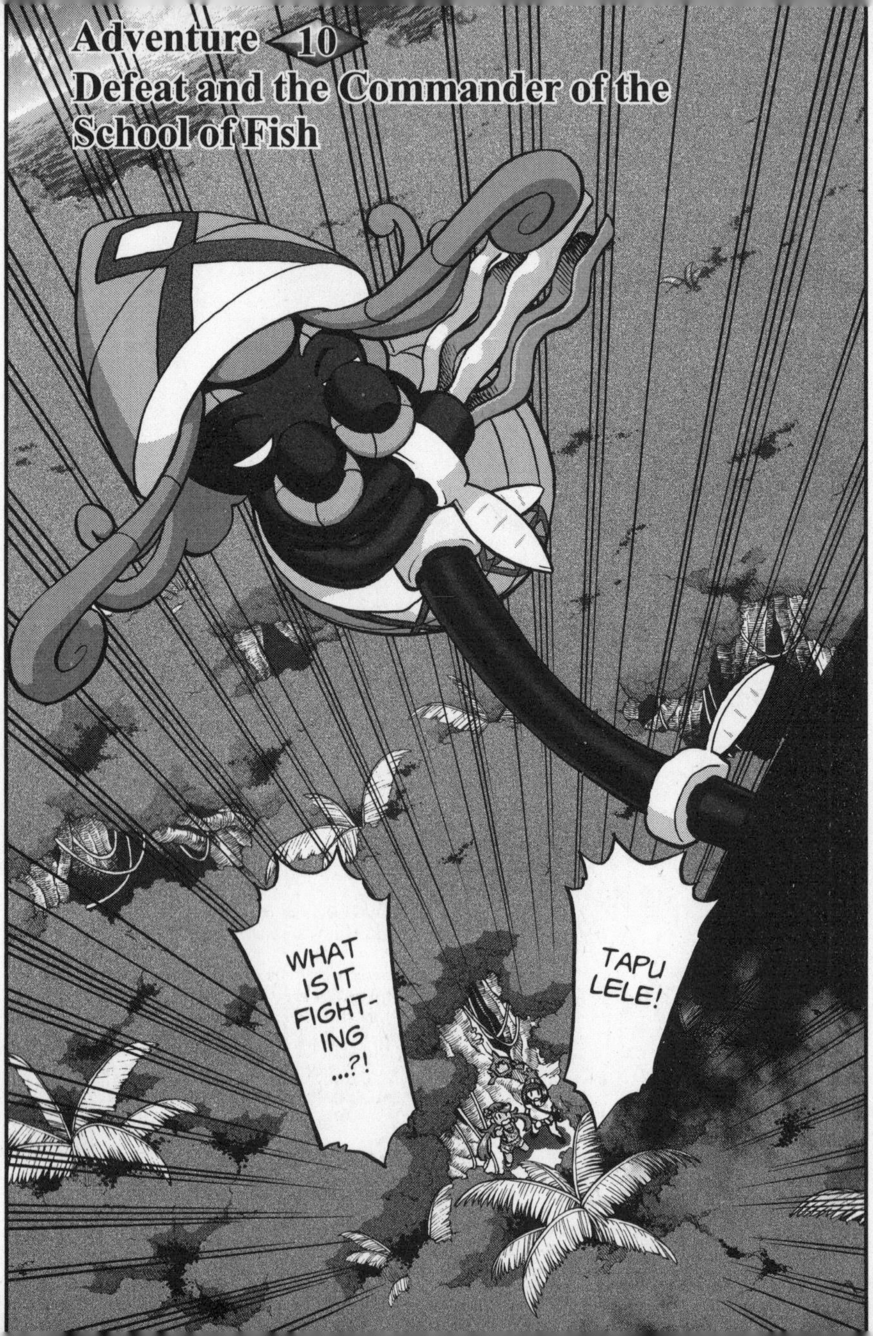

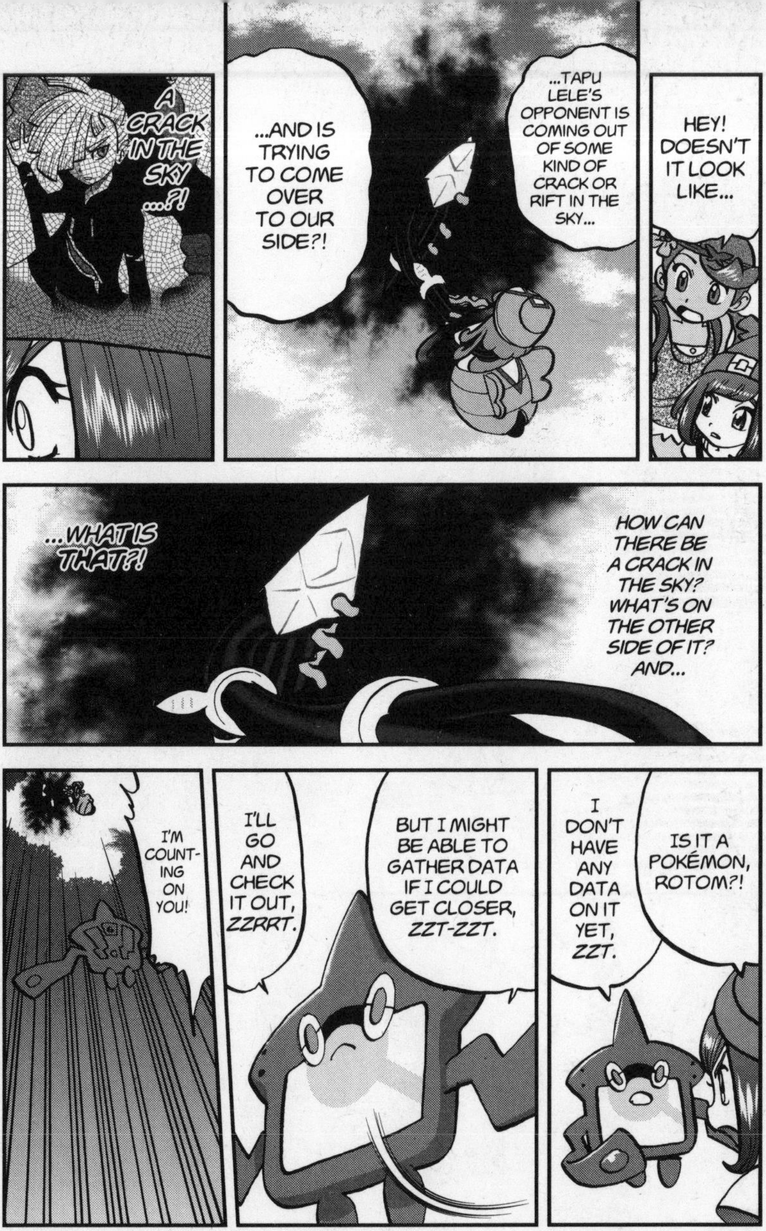
HEY! DOESN'T IT LOOK LIKE...
...TAPU LELE'S OPPONENT IS COMING OUT OF SOME KIND OF CRACK OR RIFT IN THE SKY...
...AND IS TRYING TO COME OVER TO OUR SIDE?!
A CRACK IN THE SKY ...?!
HOW CAN THERE BE A CRACK IN THE SKY? WHAT'S ON THE OTHER SIDE OF IT? AND...
...WHAT IS THAT?!
IS IT A POKÉMON, ROTOM?!
I DON'T HAVE ANY DATA ON IT YET, ZZT.
BUT I MIGHT BE ABLE TO GATHER DATA IF I COULD GET CLOSER, ZZT-ZZT.
I'LL GO AND CHECK IT OUT, ZZRRT.
I'M COUNTING ON YOU!

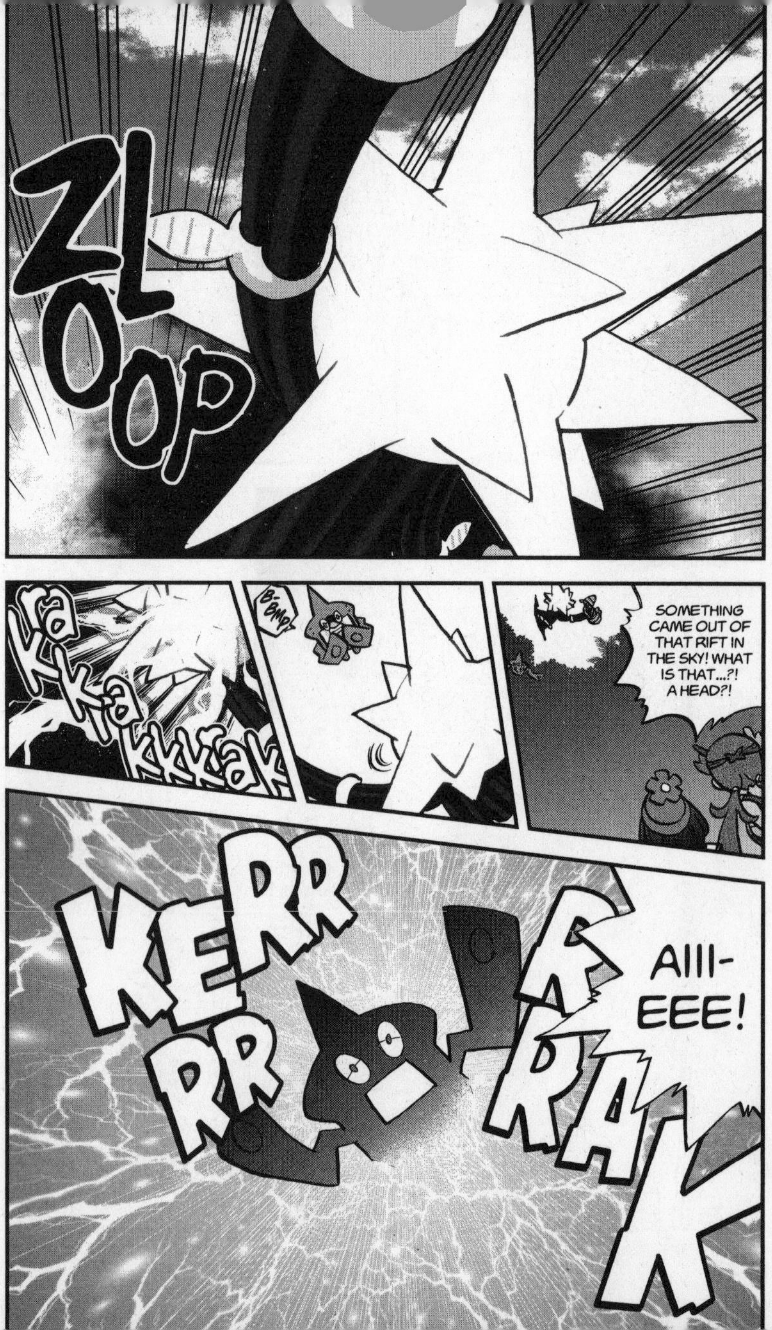
ZLOOP
SOMETHING CAME OUT OF THAT RIFT IN THE SKY! WHAT IS THAT...?! A HEAD?!
B-BMP!
KERRRR
AIII-EEE!

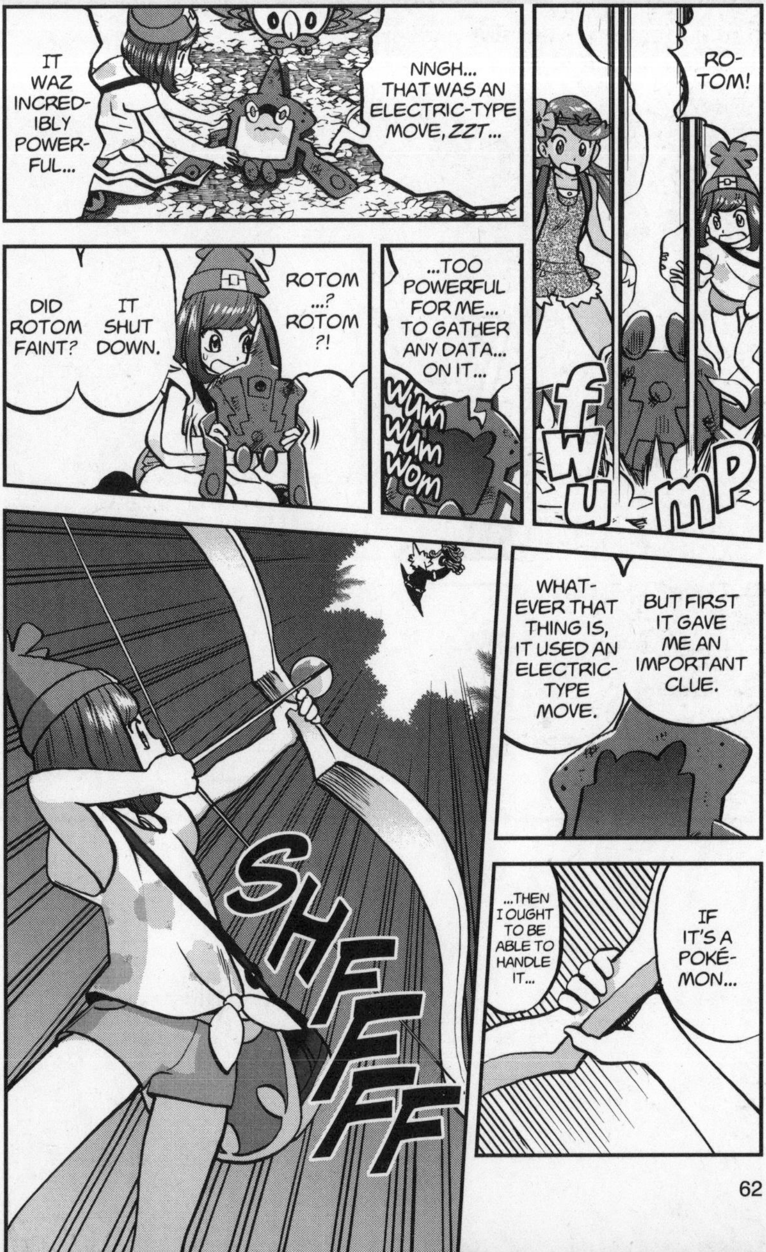
RO-TOM!
fwump
NNGH... THAT WAS AN ELECTRIC-TYPE MOVE, ZZT...
IT WAZ INCRED-IBLY POWER-FUL...
...TOO POWERFUL FOR ME... TO GATHER ANY DATA... ON IT...
wum wum wom
ROTOM ...? ROTOM ?!
IT SHUT DOWN.
DID ROTOM FAINT?
BUT FIRST IT GAVE ME AN IMPORTANT CLUE.
WHAT-EVER THAT THING IS, IT USED AN ELECTRIC-TYPE MOVE.
IF IT'S A POKÉ-MON...
...THEN I OUGHT TO BE ABLE TO HANDLE IT...
SHFFFFF

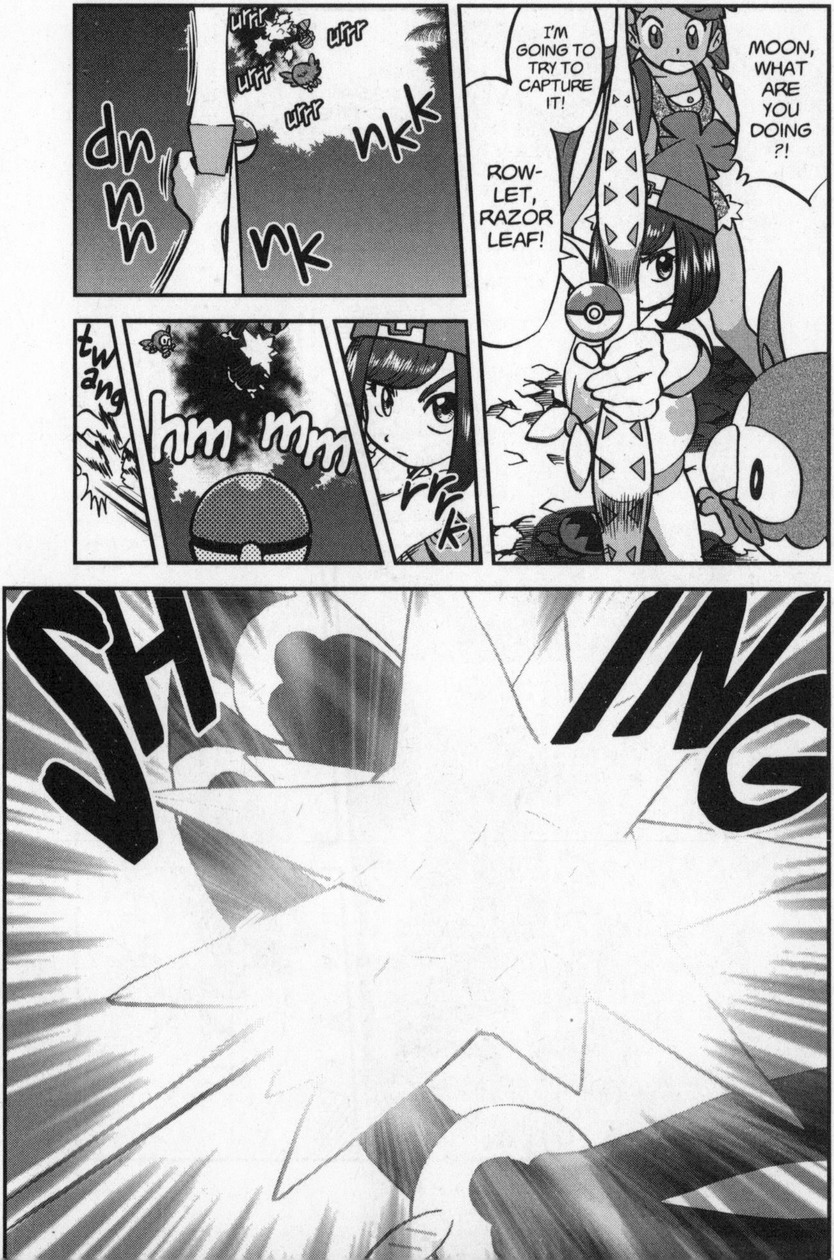
MOON, WHAT ARE YOU DOING?!
I'M GOING TO TRY TO CAPTURE IT!
ROW-LET, RAZOR LEAF!
urrr
urrr
urrr
urrr
nkk
dnnn
nk
rrrk
hm mm
twang
SHING

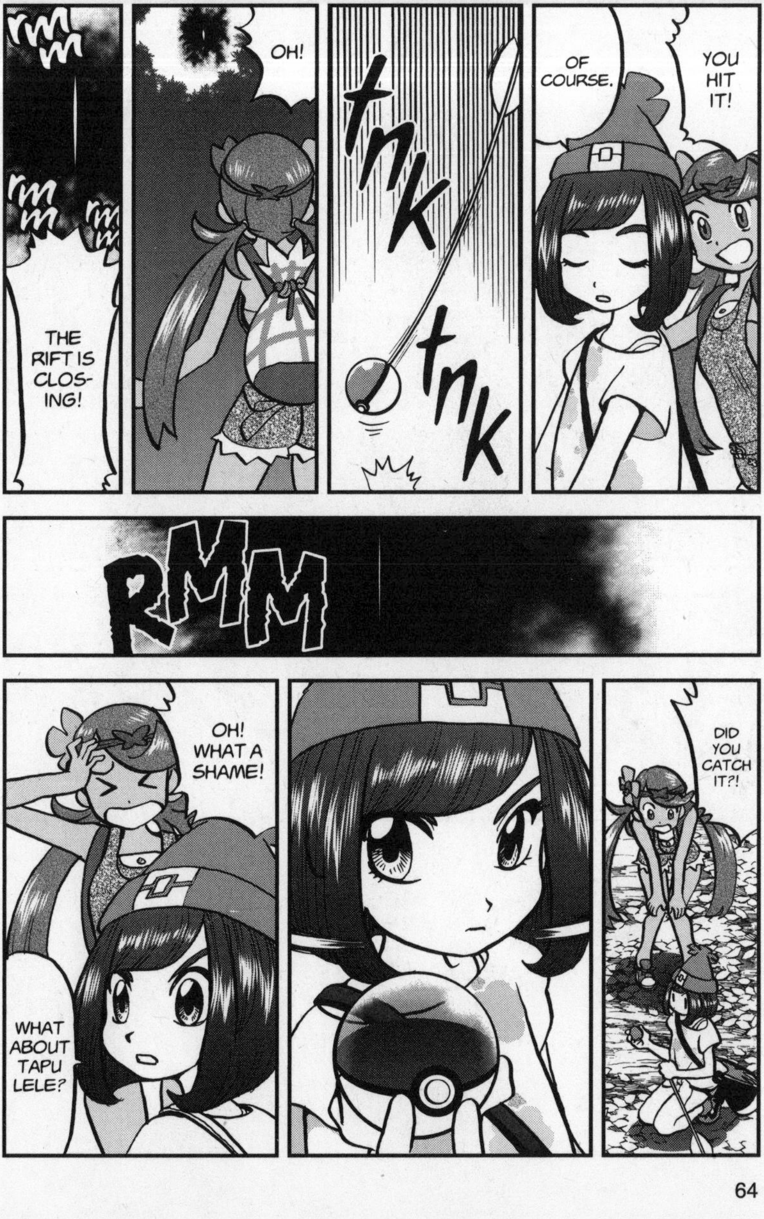
YOU HIT IT!
OF COURSE.
tnk
tnk
OH!
rmm
rmm
rmm
rmm
THE RIFT IS CLOSING!
RMM
DID YOU CATCH IT?!
OH! WHAT A SHAME!
WHAT ABOUT TAPU LELE?

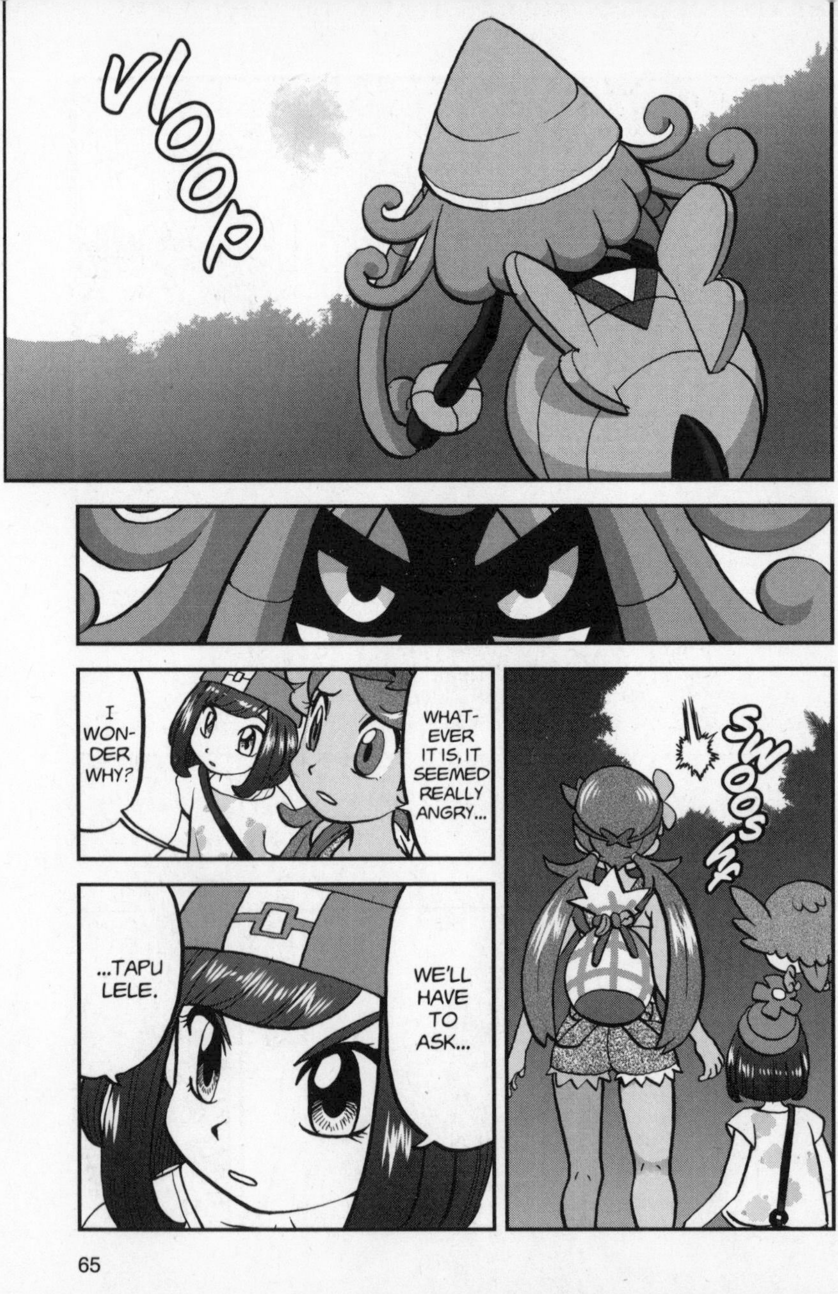
VLOOP
SWOOSH
WHAT-EVER IT IS, IT SEEMED REALLY ANGRY...
I WON-DER WHY?
WE'LL HAVE TO ASK...
...TAPU LELE.

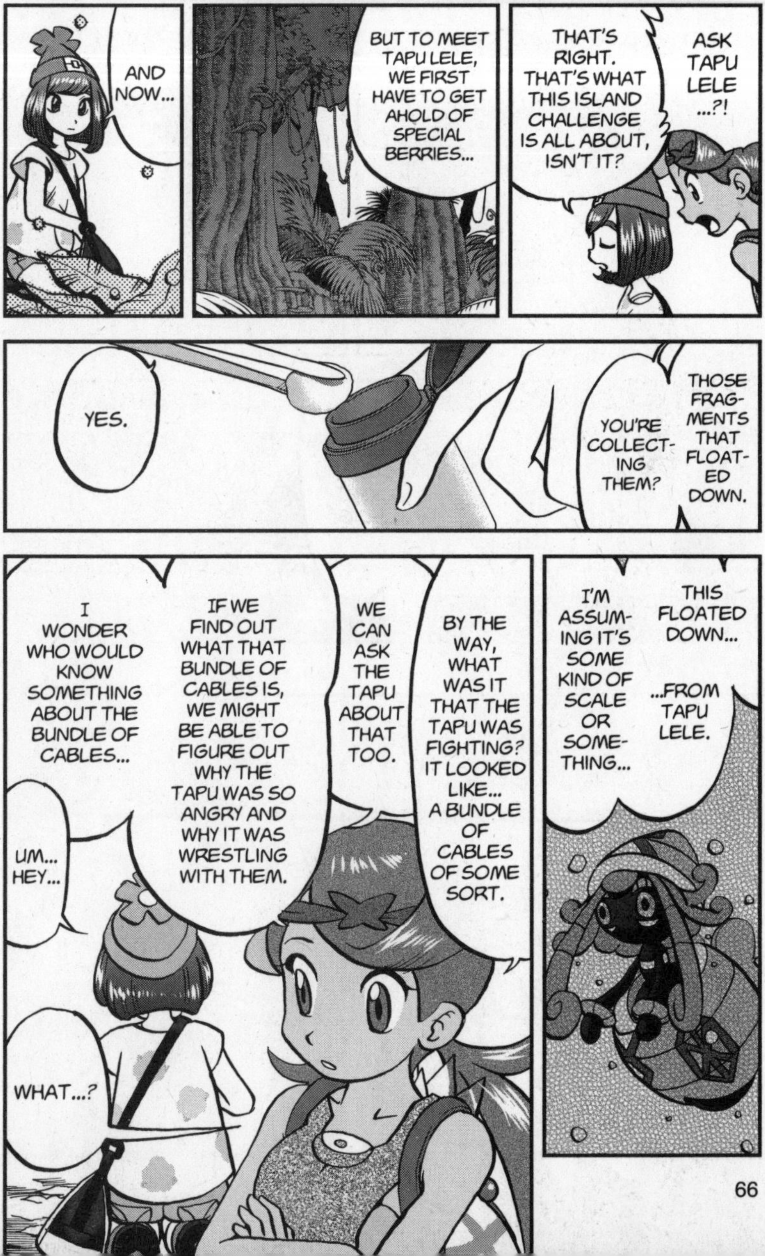
ASK TAPU LELE ...?!
THAT'S RIGHT. THAT'S WHAT THIS ISLAND CHALLENGE IS ALL ABOUT, ISN'T IT?
BUT TO MEET TAPU LELE, WE FIRST HAVE TO GET AHOLD OF SPECIAL BERRIES...
AND NOW...
THOSE FRAG-MENTS THAT FLOAT-ED DOWN.
YOU'RE COLLECT-ING THEM?
YES.
THIS FLOATED DOWN...
...FROM TAPU LELE.
I'M ASSUM-ING IT'S SOME KIND OF SCALE OR SOME-THING...
BY THE WAY, WHAT WAS IT THAT THE TAPU WAS FIGHTING? IT LOOKED LIKE... A BUNDLE OF CABLES OF SOME SORT.
WE CAN ASK THE TAPU ABOUT THAT TOO.
IF WE FIND OUT WHAT THAT BUNDLE OF CABLES IS, WE MIGHT BE ABLE TO FIGURE OUT WHY THE TAPU WAS SO ANGRY AND WHY IT WAS WRESTLING WITH THEM.
I WONDER WHO WOULD KNOW SOMETHING ABOUT THE BUNDLE OF CABLES...
UM... HEY...
WHAT...?

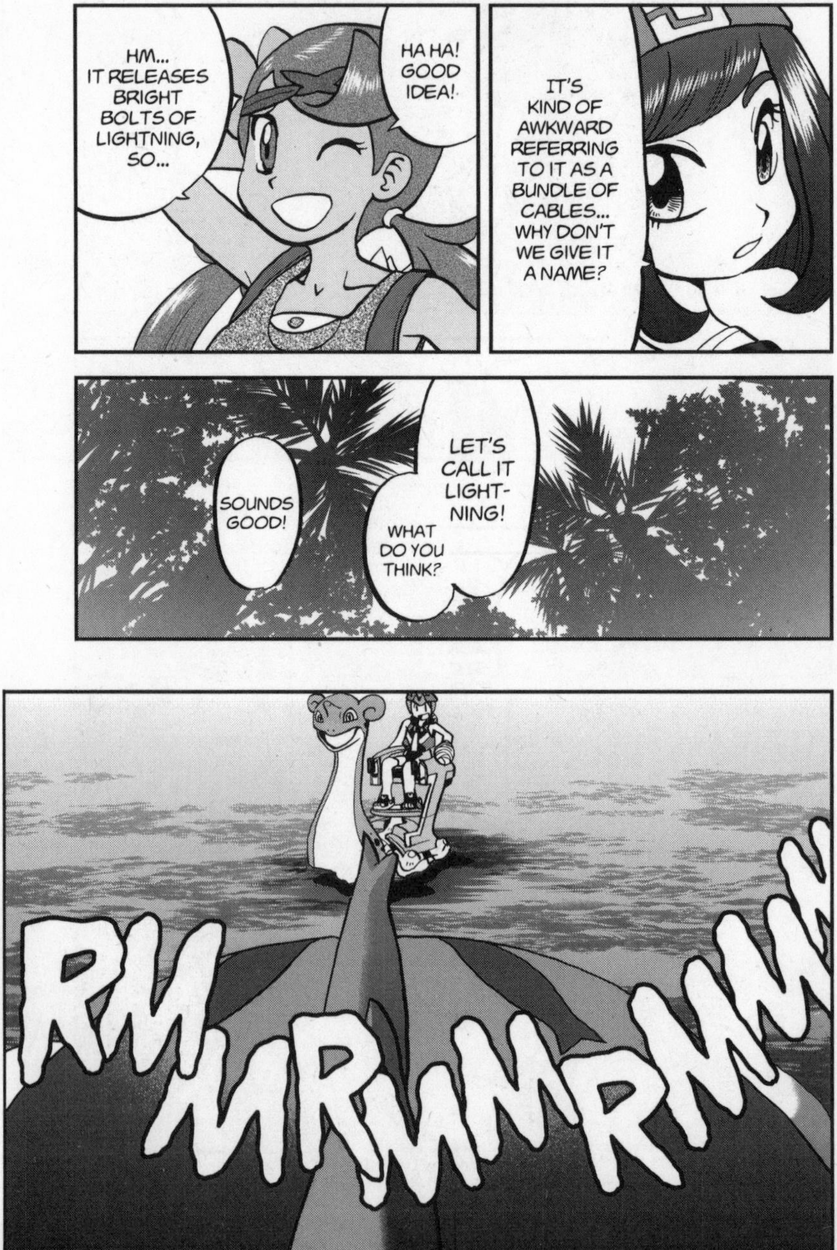
IT'S KIND OF AWKWARD REFERRING TO IT AS A BUNDLE OF CABLES... WHY DON'T WE GIVE IT A NAME?
HA HA! GOOD IDEA!
HM... IT RELEASES BRIGHT BOLTS OF LIGHTNING, SO...
LET'S CALL IT LIGHT-NING!
WHAT DO YOU THINK?
SOUNDS GOOD!
RMMRMMMRMMM

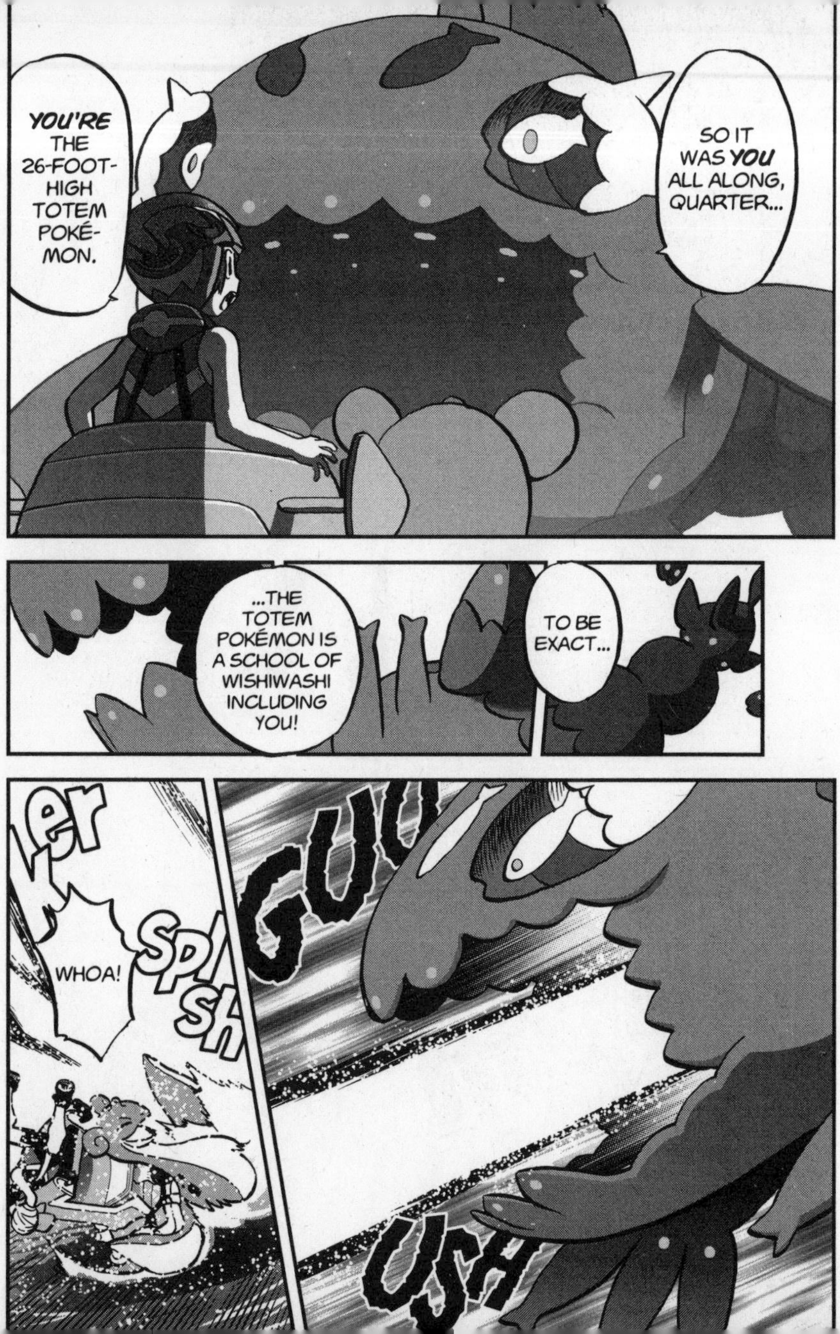
SO IT WAS YOU ALL ALONG, QUARTER...
YOU'RE THE 26-FOOT-HIGH TOTEM POKÉMON.
TO BE EXACT...
...THE TOTEM POKÉMON IS A SCHOOL OF WISHIWASHI INCLUDING YOU!
GUU
USH
SPL
SH
WHOA!
ler

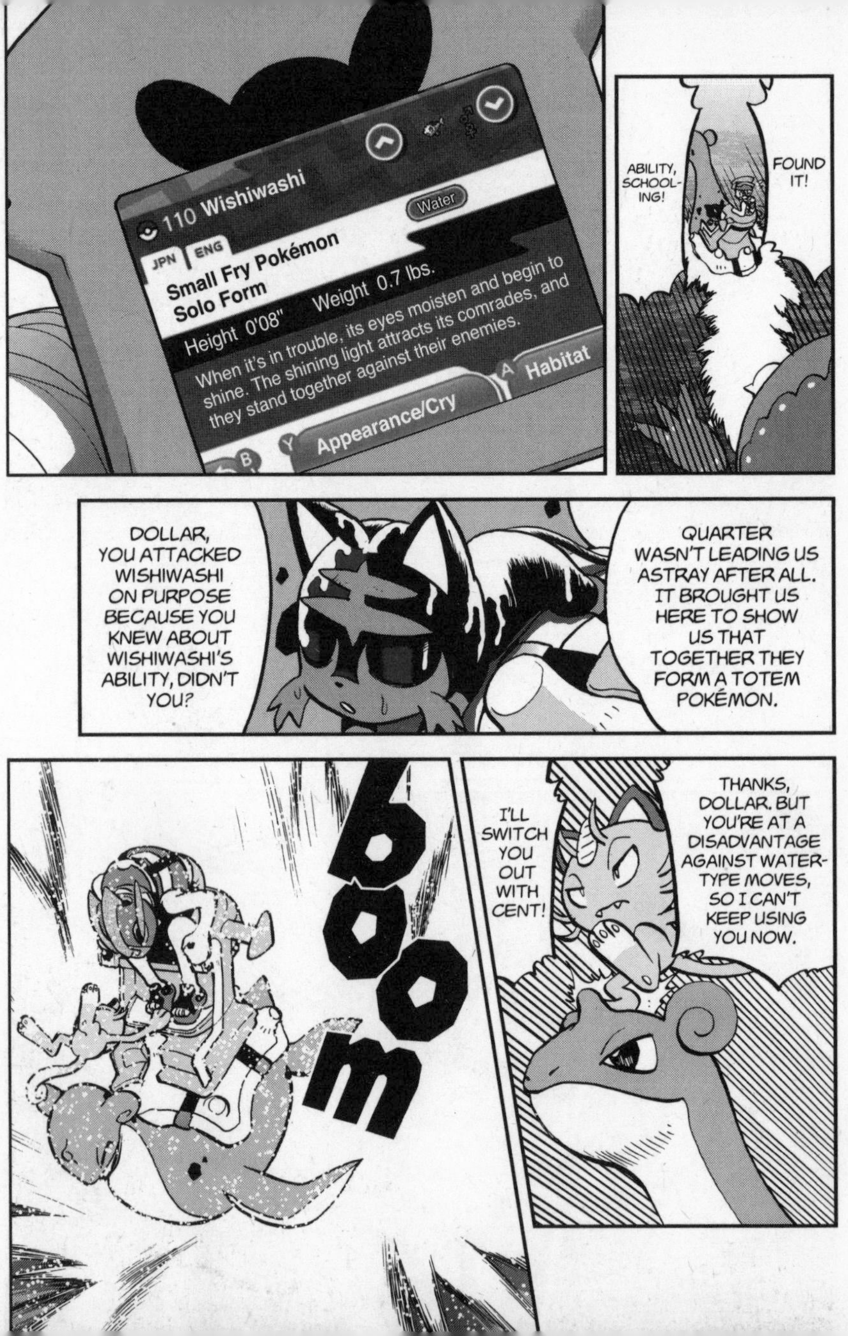
FOUND IT!
ABILITY, SCHOOL-ING!
110 Wishiwashi
Water
JPN
ENG
Small Fry Pokémon
Solo Form
Height 0'08" Weight 0.7 lbs.
When it's in trouble, its eyes moisten and begin to shine. The shining light attracts its comrades, and they stand together against their enemies.
Habitat
Appearance/Cry
QUARTER WASN'T LEADING US ASTRAY AFTER ALL. IT BROUGHT US HERE TO SHOW US THAT TOGETHER THEY FORM A TOTEM POKÉMON.
DOLLAR, YOU ATTACKED WISHIWASHI ON PURPOSE BECAUSE YOU KNEW ABOUT WISHIWASHI'S ABILITY, DIDN'T YOU?
THANKS, DOLLAR. BUT YOU'RE AT A DISADVANTAGE AGAINST WATER-TYPE MOVES, SO I CAN'T KEEP USING YOU NOW.
I'LL SWITCH YOU OUT WITH CENT!
booom

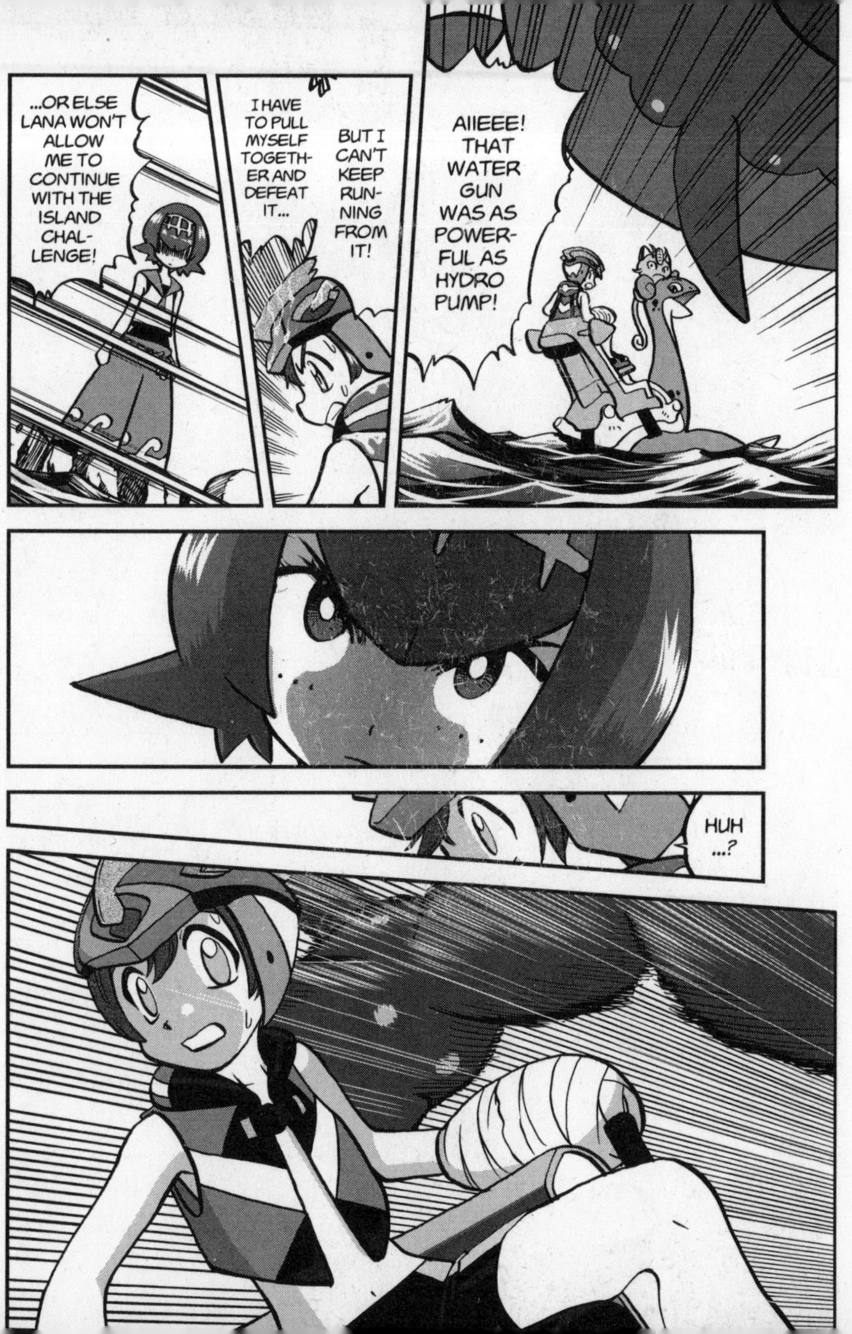
AIIEEE! THAT WATER GUN WAS AS POWERFUL AS HYDRO PUMP!
BUT I CAN'T KEEP RUNNING FROM IT!
I HAVE TO PULL MYSELF TOGETHER AND DEFEAT IT...
...OR ELSE LANA WON'T ALLOW ME TO CONTINUE WITH THE ISLAND CHALLENGE!
HUH...?

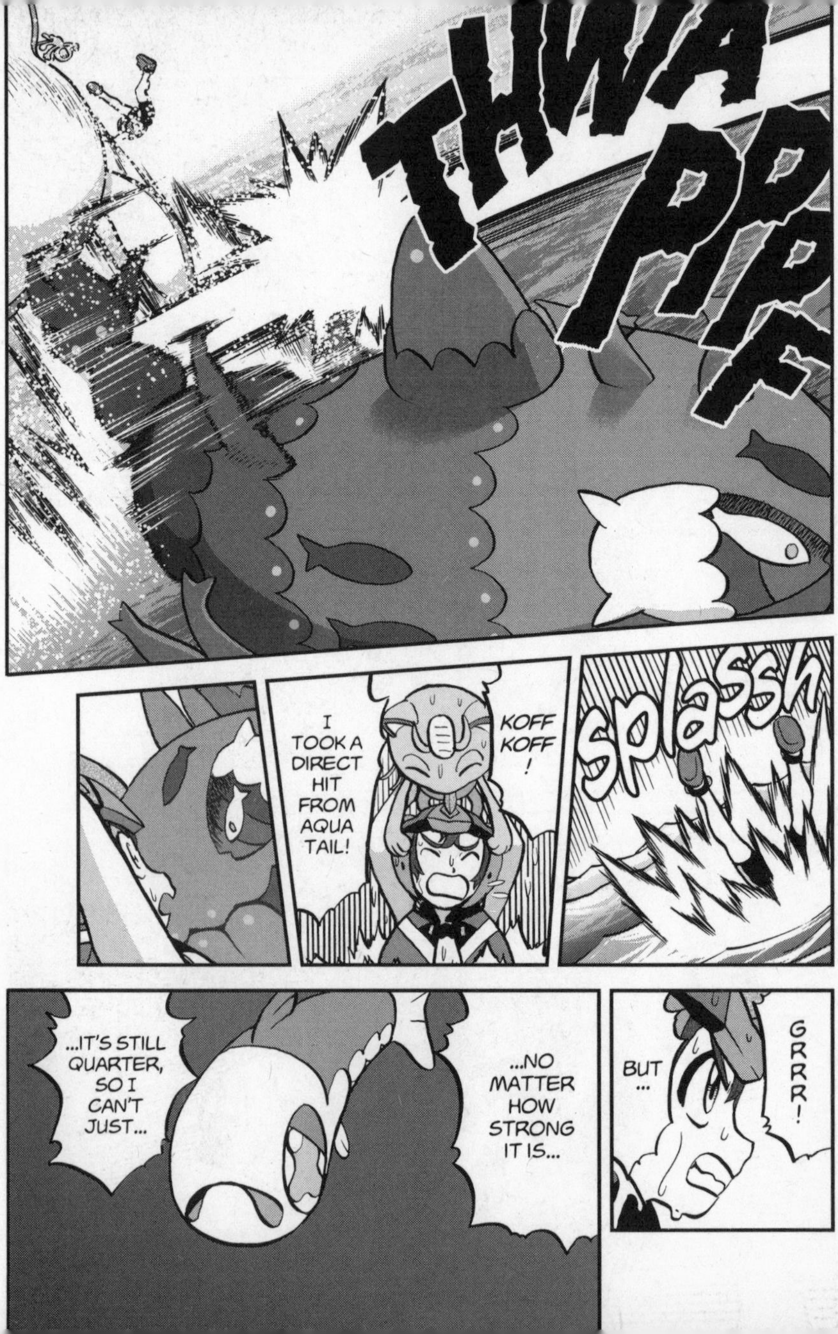
THWAPPPF
splassh
KOFF KOFF!
I TOOK A DIRECT HIT FROM AQUA TAIL!
GRRR!
BUT...
...NO MATTER HOW STRONG IT IS...
...IT'S STILL QUARTER, SO I CAN'T JUST...

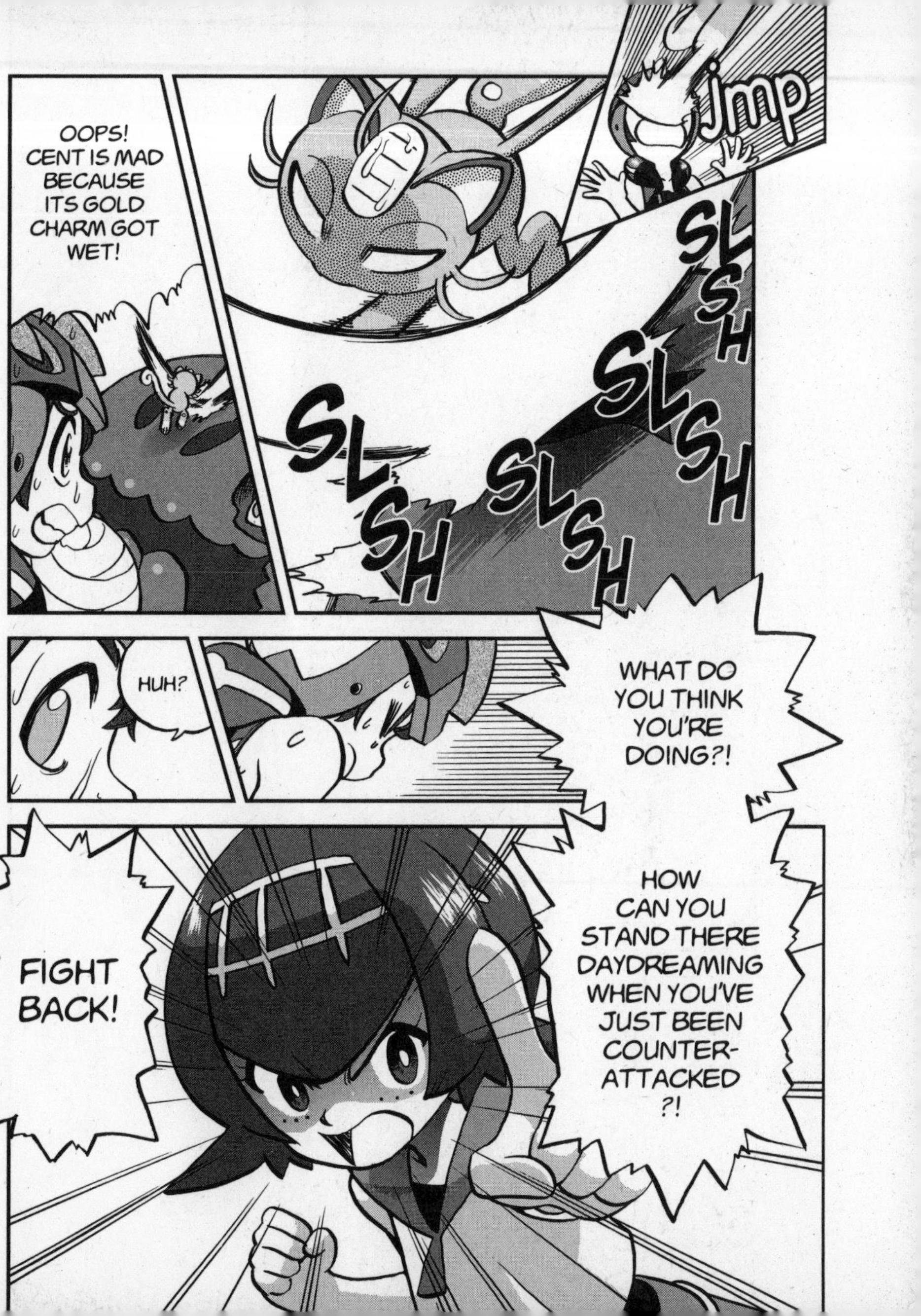
jmp
SLSH
SLSH
SLSH
SLSH
OOPS! CENT IS MAD BECAUSE ITS GOLD CHARM GOT WET!
WHAT DO YOU THINK YOU'RE DOING?!
HUH?
HOW CAN YOU STAND THERE DAYDREAMING WHEN YOU'VE JUST BEEN COUNTER-ATTACKED?!
FIGHT BACK!

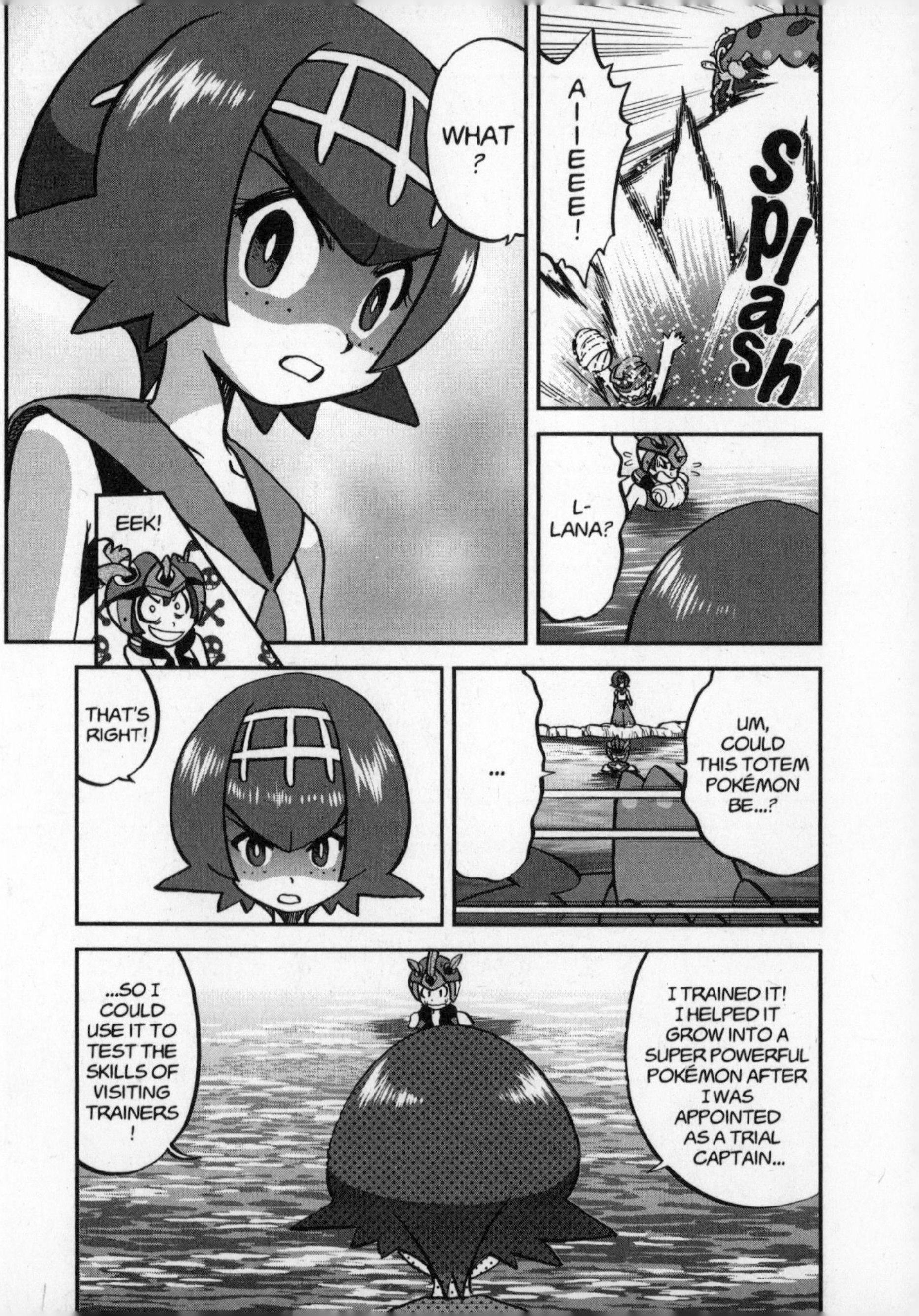
A-IIEEE!
Splash
L-LANA?
WHAT?
EEK!
UM, COULD THIS TOTEM POKÉMON BE...?
...
THAT'S RIGHT!
I TRAINED IT! I HELPED IT GROW INTO A SUPER POWERFUL POKÉMON AFTER I WAS APPOINTED AS A TRIAL CAPTAIN...
...SO I COULD USE IT TO TEST THE SKILLS OF VISITING TRAINERS!

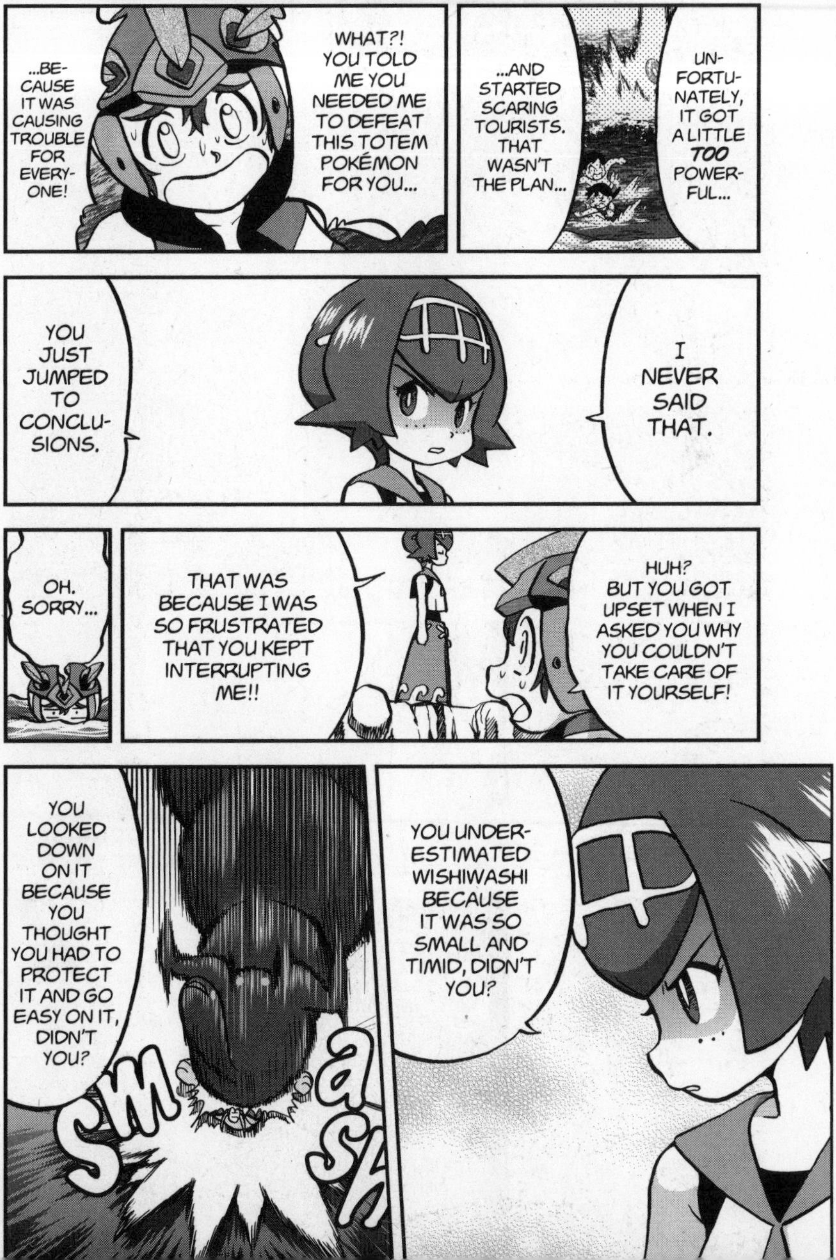
UN-FORTU-NATELY, IT GOT A LITTLE TOO POWER-FUL...
...AND STARTED SCARING TOURISTS. THAT WASN'T THE PLAN...
WHAT?! YOU TOLD ME YOU NEEDED ME TO DEFEAT THIS TOTEM POKÉMON FOR YOU...
...BE-CAUSE IT WAS CAUSING TROUBLE FOR EVERY-ONE!
I NEVER SAID THAT.
YOU JUST JUMPED TO CONCLU-SIONS.
HUH? BUT YOU GOT UPSET WHEN I ASKED YOU WHY YOU COULDN'T TAKE CARE OF IT YOURSELF!
THAT WAS BECAUSE I WAS SO FRUSTRATED THAT YOU KEPT INTERRUPTING ME!!
OH. SORRY...
YOU UNDER-ESTIMATED WISHIWASHI BECAUSE IT WAS SO SMALL AND TIMID, DIDN'T YOU?
YOU LOOKED DOWN ON IT BECAUSE YOU THOUGHT YOU HAD TO PROTECT IT AND GO EASY ON IT, DIDN'T YOU?
SMASH

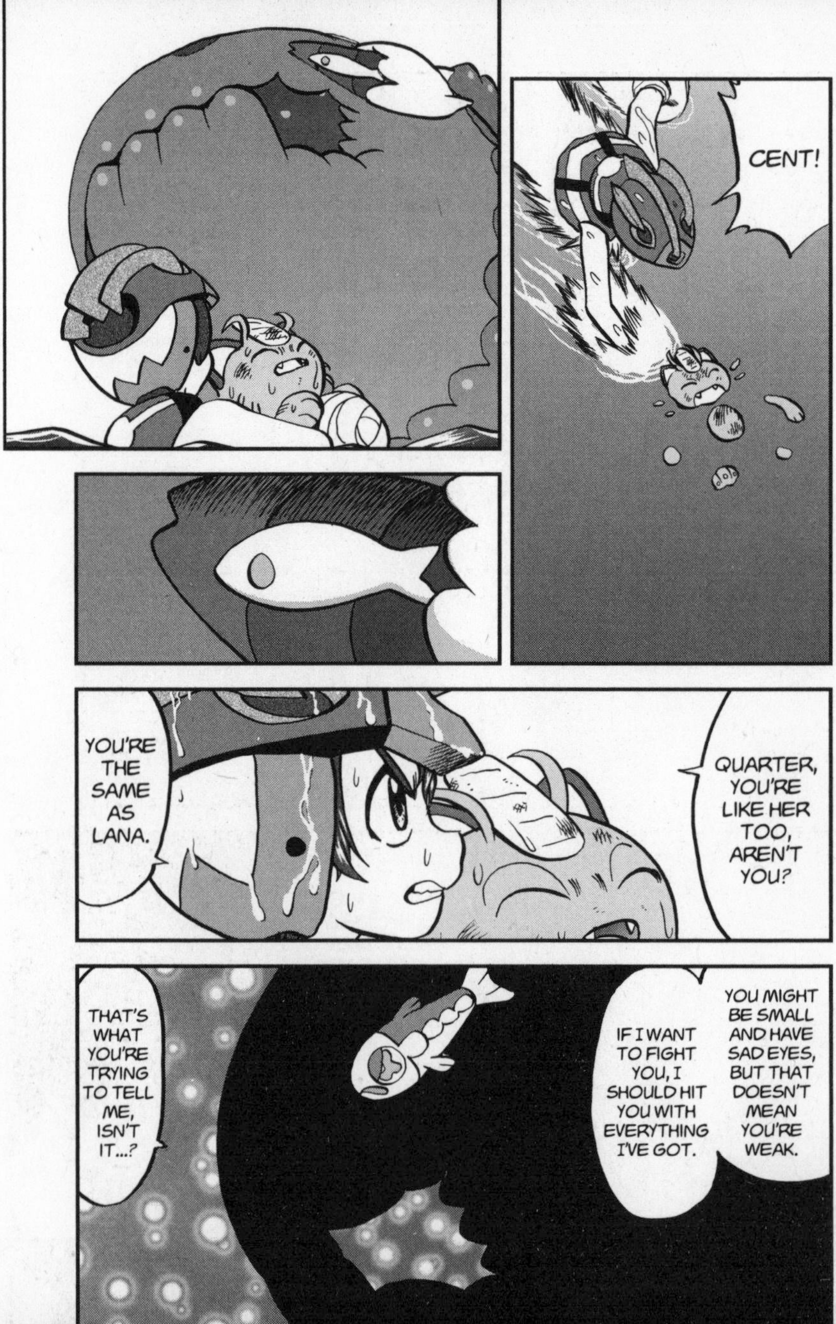
CENT!
QUARTER, YOU'RE LIKE HER TOO, AREN'T YOU?
YOU'RE THE SAME AS LANA.
YOU MIGHT BE SMALL AND HAVE SAD EYES, BUT THAT DOESN'T MEAN YOU'RE WEAK.
IF I WANT TO FIGHT YOU, I SHOULD HIT YOU WITH EVERYTHING I'VE GOT.
THAT'S WHAT YOU'RE TRYING TO TELL ME, ISN'T IT...?

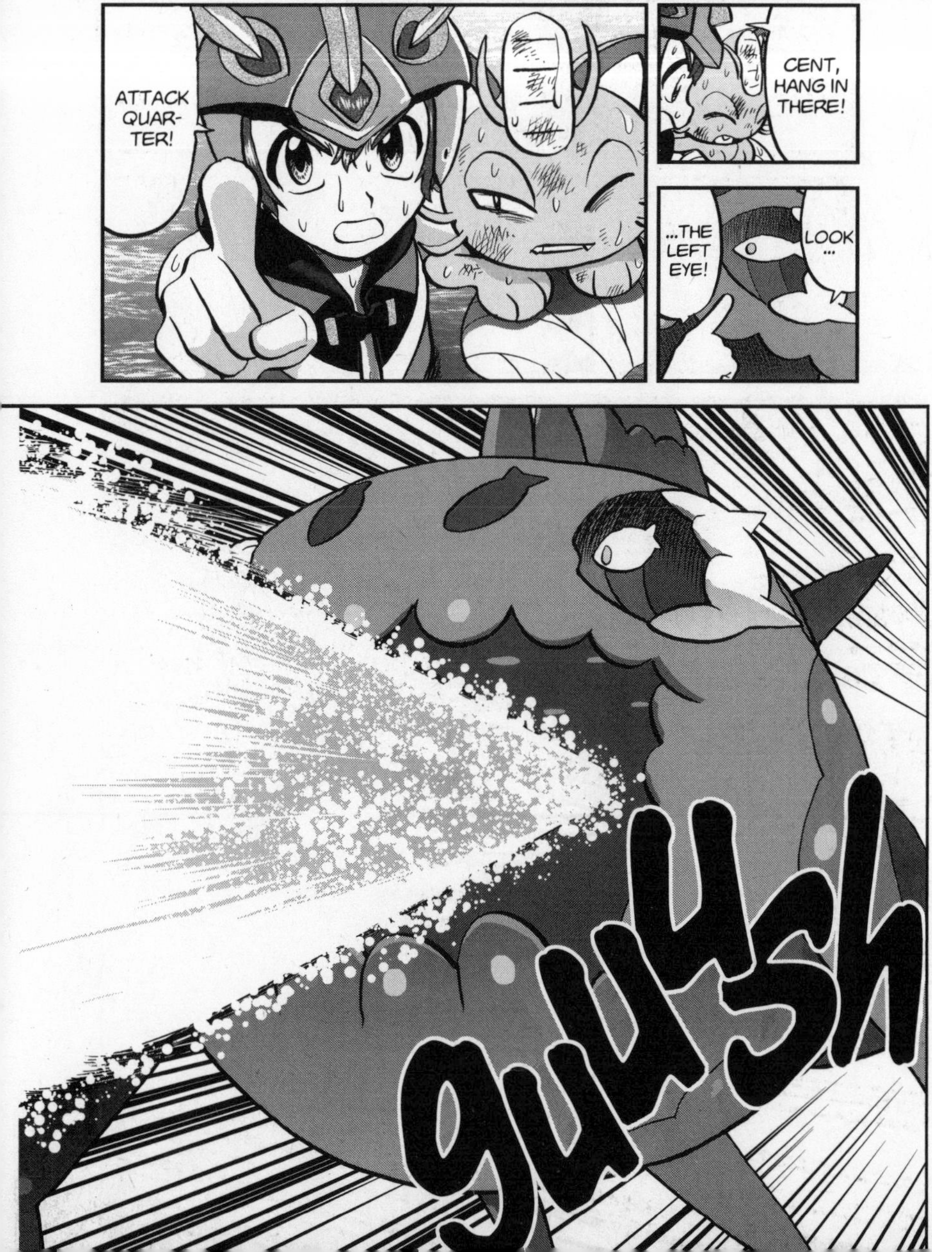
CENT, HANG IN THERE!
LOOK...
...THE LEFT EYE!
ATTACK QUAR-TER!
guuush

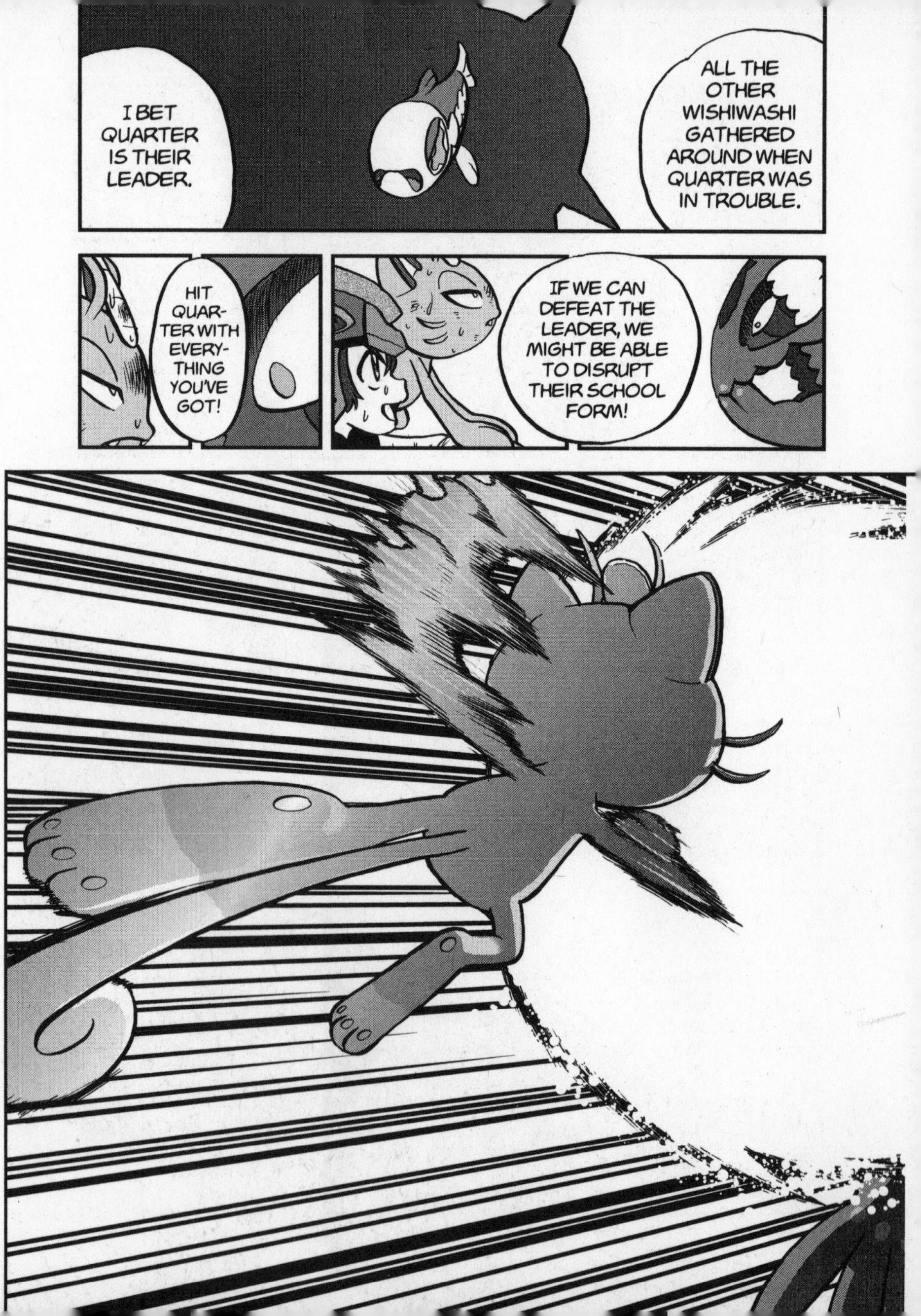
ALL THE OTHER WISHIWASHI GATHERED AROUND WHEN QUARTER WAS IN TROUBLE.
I BET QUARTER IS THEIR LEADER.
IF WE CAN DEFEAT THE LEADER, WE MIGHT BE ABLE TO DISRUPT THEIR SCHOOL FORM!
HIT QUARTER WITH EVERYTHING YOU'VE GOT!

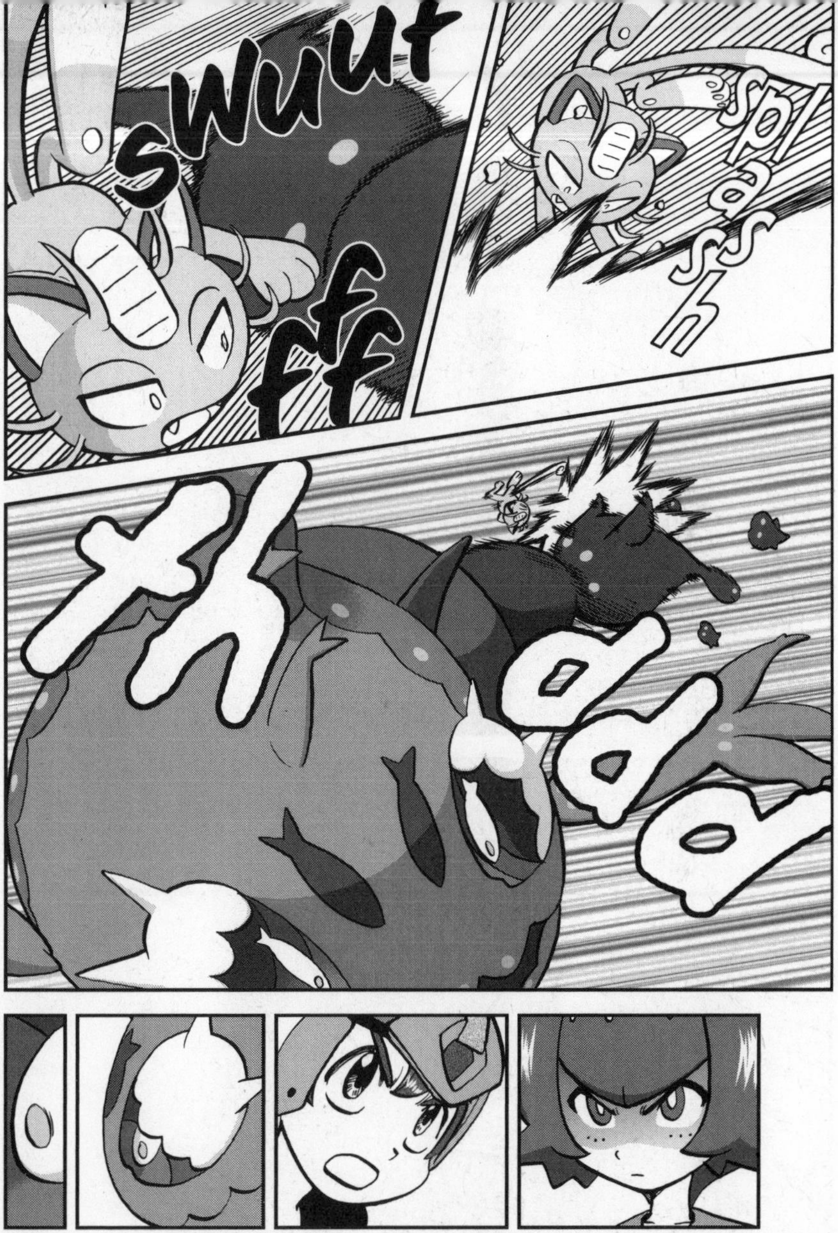
splash
swuut
fff

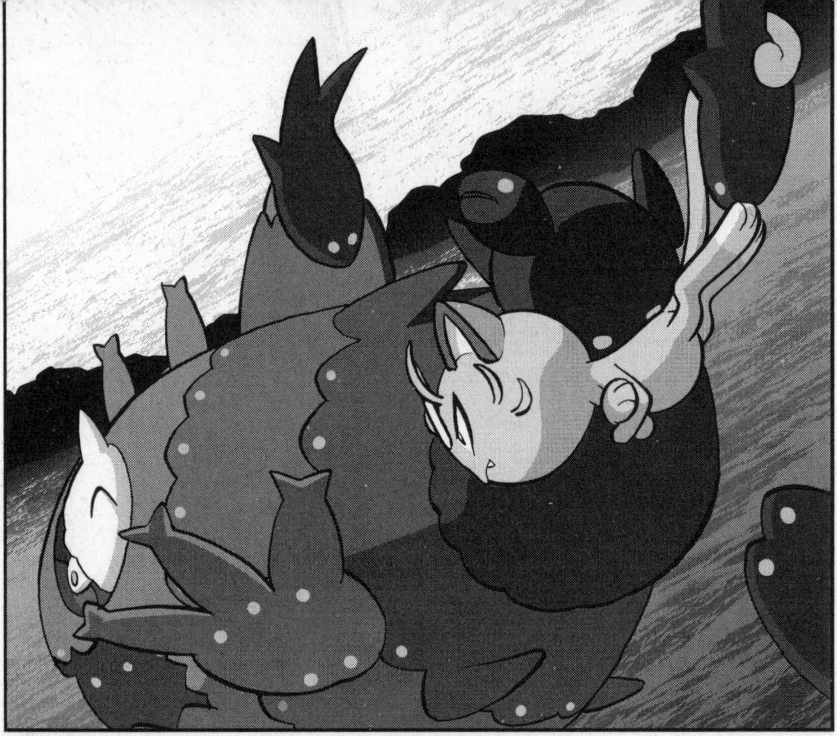

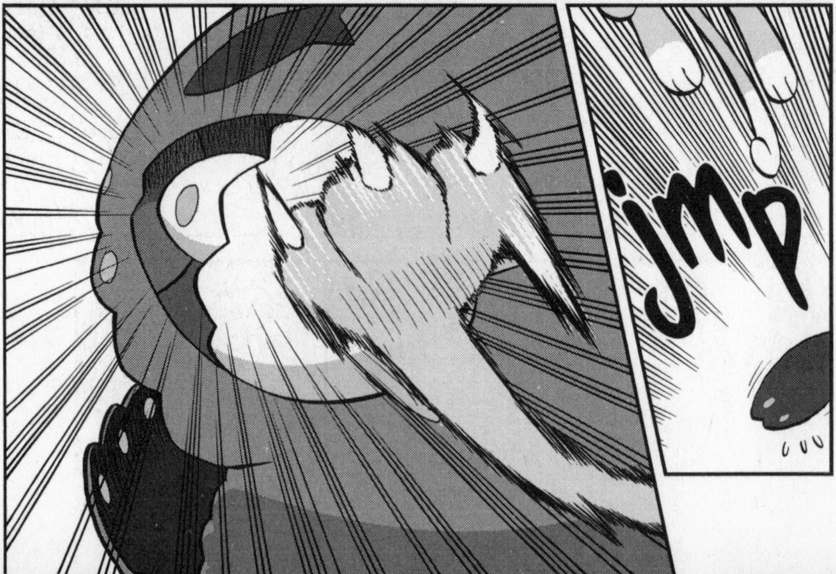
jmp

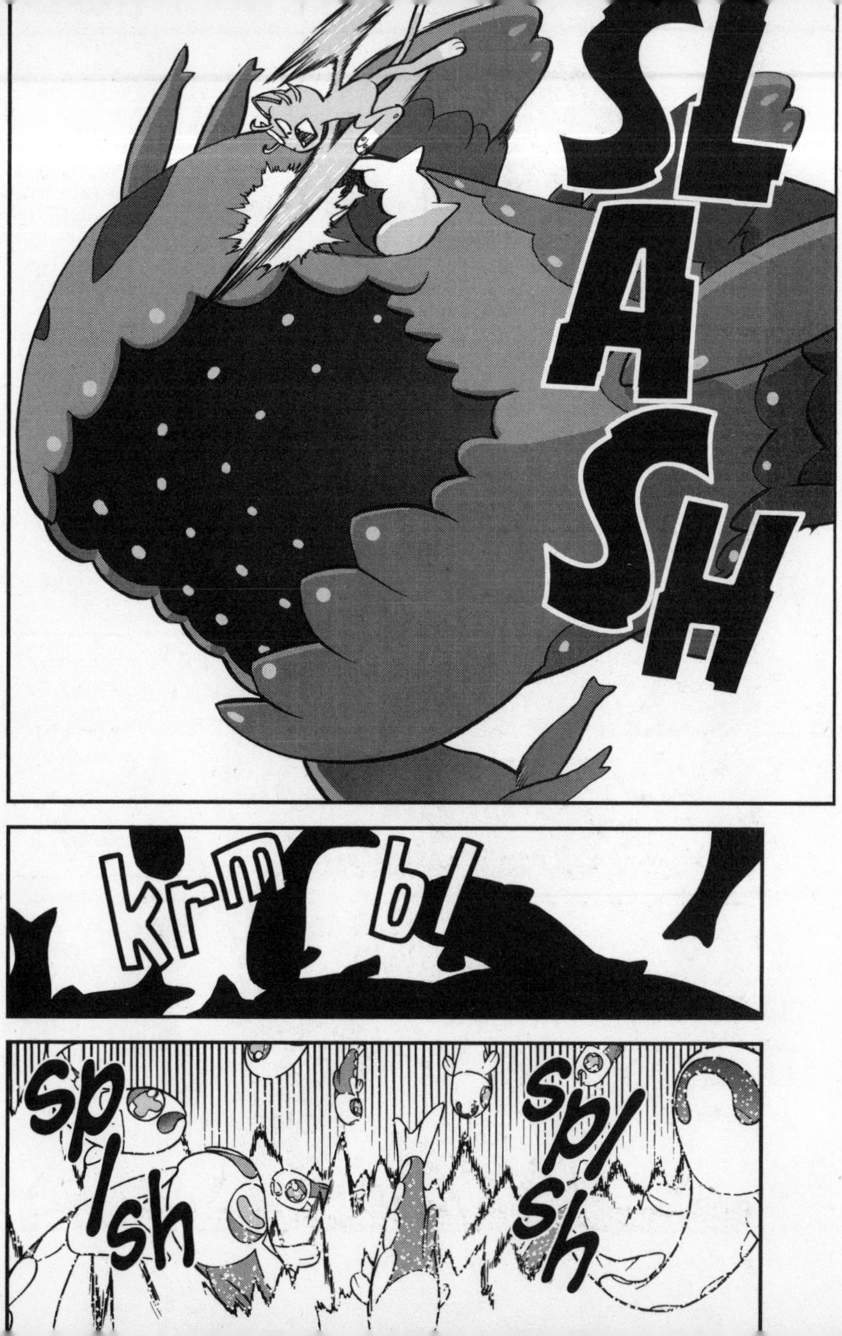
SLASH
krmbl
splsh
splsh

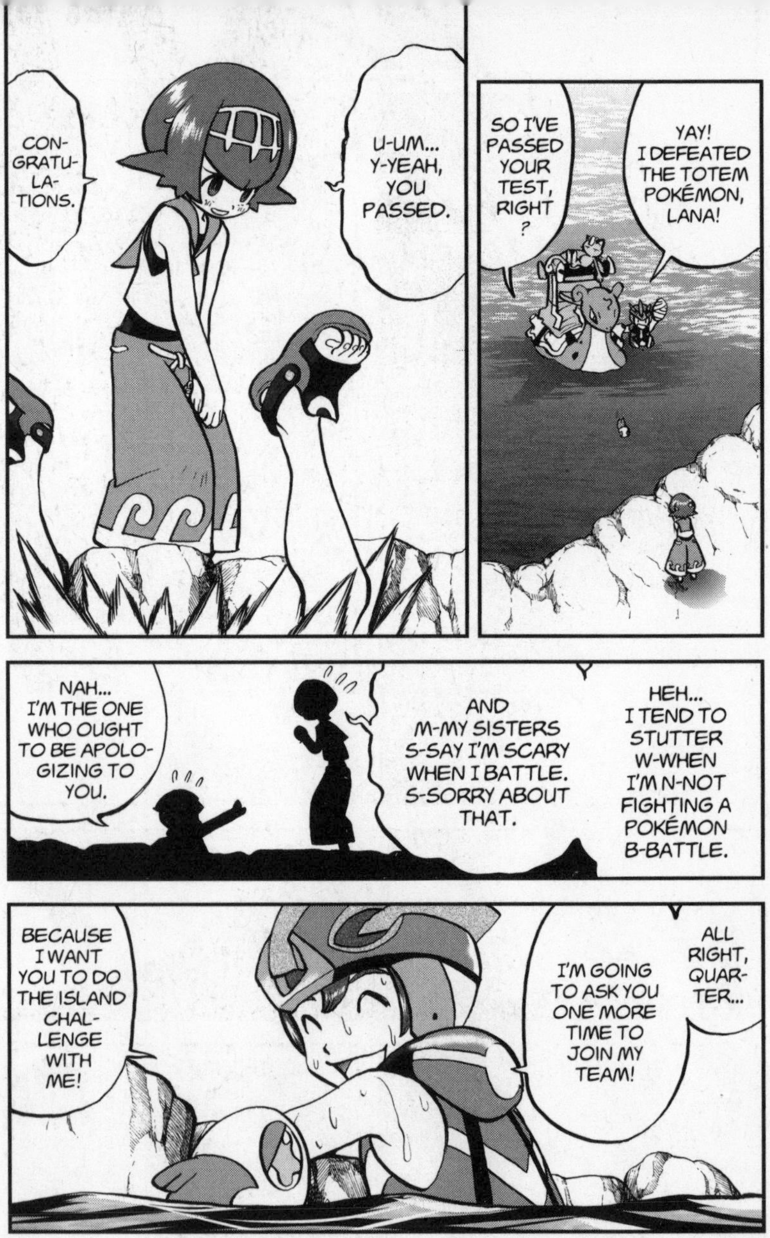
YAY! I DEFEATED THE TOTEM POKÉMON, LANA!
SO I'VE PASSED YOUR TEST, RIGHT?
U-UM... Y-YEAH, YOU PASSED.
CONGRATULATIONS.
HEH... I TEND TO STUTTER W-WHEN I'M N-NOT FIGHTING A POKÉMON B-BATTLE.
AND M-MY SISTERS S-SAY I'M SCARY WHEN I BATTLE. S-SORRY ABOUT THAT.
NAH... I'M THE ONE WHO OUGHT TO BE APOLOGIZING TO YOU.
ALL RIGHT, QUARTER...
I'M GOING TO ASK YOU ONE MORE TIME TO JOIN MY TEAM!
BECAUSE I WANT YOU TO DO THE ISLAND CHALLENGE WITH ME!

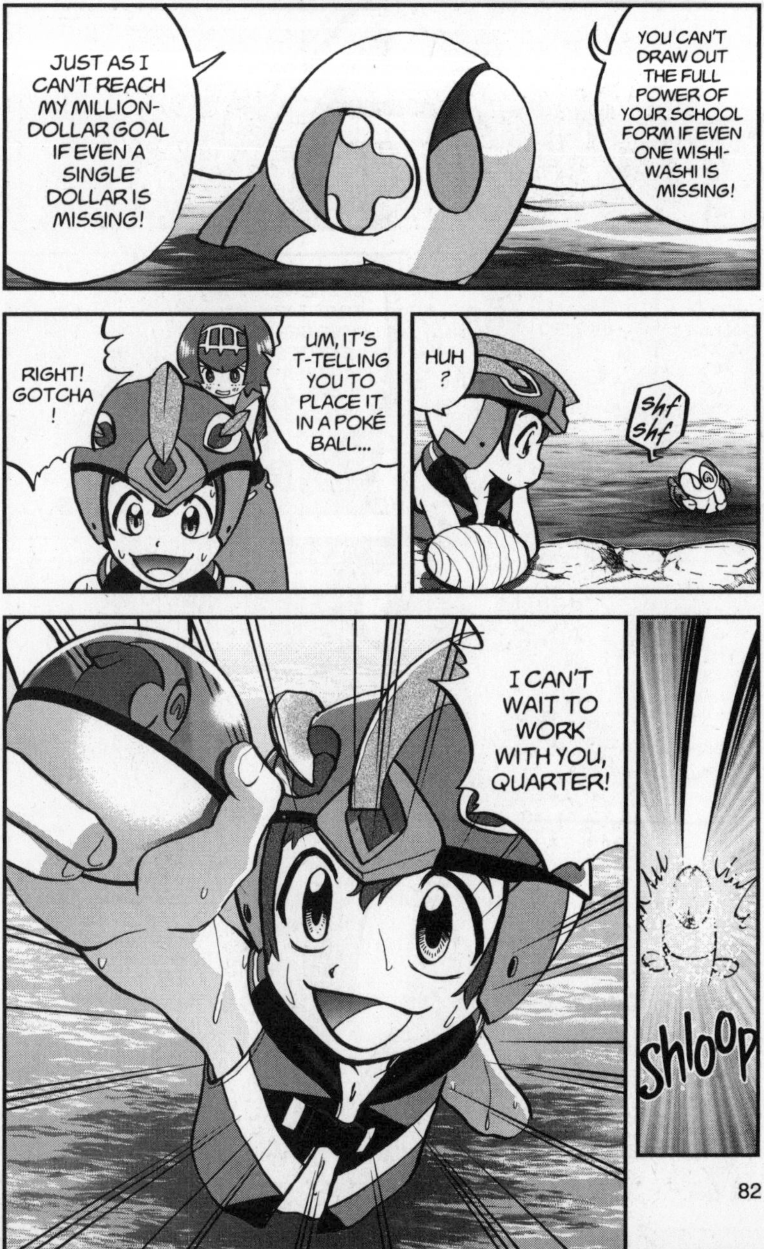
YOU CAN'T DRAW OUT THE FULL POWER OF YOUR SCHOOL FORM IF EVEN ONE WISHI-WASHI IS MISSING!
JUST AS I CAN'T REACH MY MILLION-DOLLAR GOAL IF EVEN A SINGLE DOLLAR IS MISSING!
shf shf
HUH ?
UM, IT'S T-TELLING YOU TO PLACE IT IN A POKÉ BALL...
RIGHT! GOTCHA !
shloop
I CAN'T WAIT TO WORK WITH YOU, QUARTER!

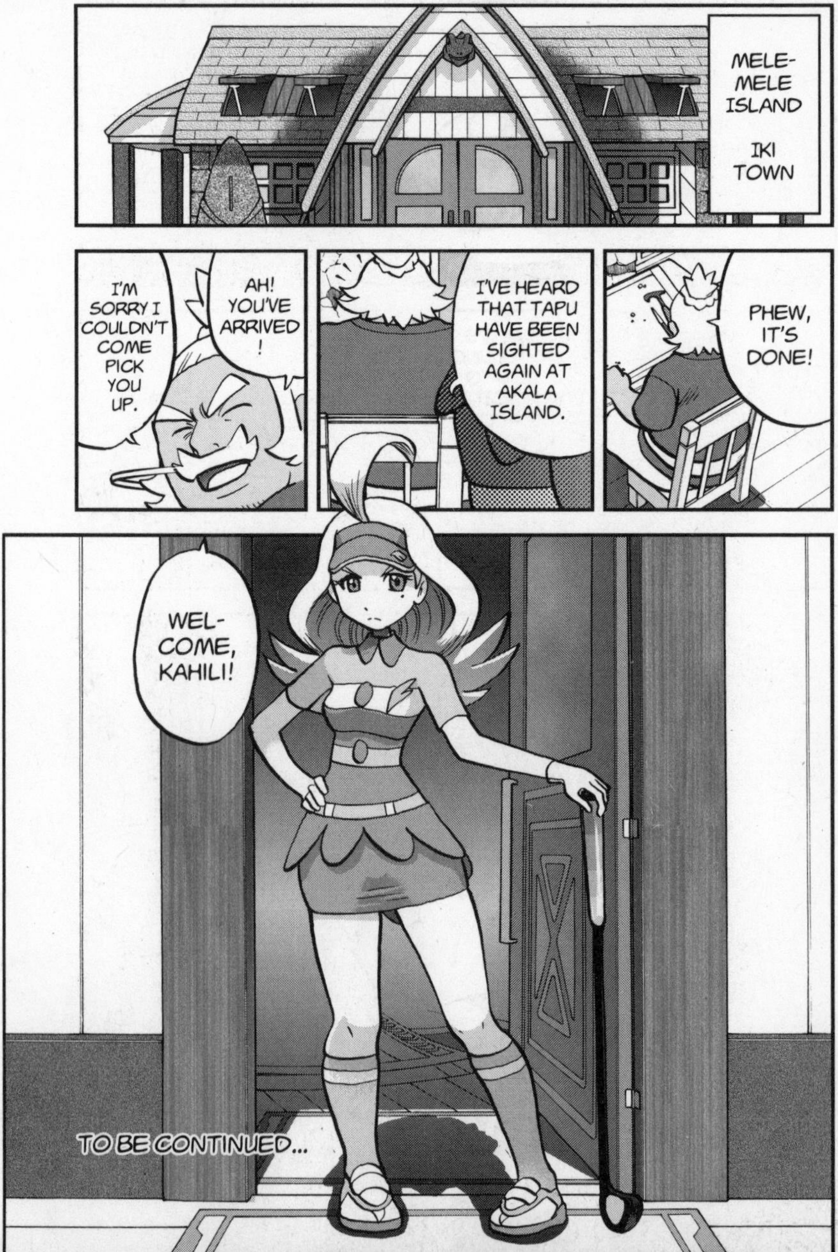
MELE-MELE ISLAND
IKI TOWN
PHEW, IT'S DONE!
I'VE HEARD THAT TAPU HAVE BEEN SIGHTED AGAIN AT AKALA ISLAND.
AH! YOU'VE ARRIVED!
I'M SORRY I COULDN'T COME PICK YOU UP.
WEL-COME, KAHILI!
TO BE CONTINUED...

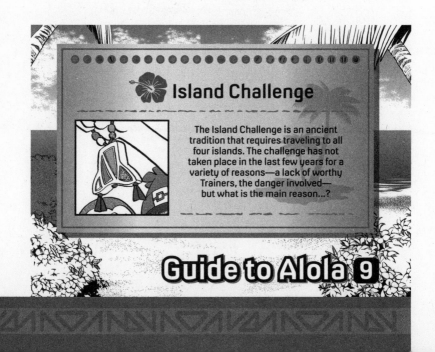

Island Challenge

The Island Challenge is an ancient tradition that requires traveling to all four islands. The challenge has not taken place in the last few years for a variety of reasons—a lack of worthy Trainers, the danger involved— but what is the main reason...?

Guide to Alola 9

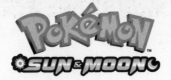

Pokémon Sun & Moon
Volume 3
VIZ Media Edition

Story by HIDENORI KUSAKA
Art by SATOSHI YAMAMOTO

©2019 The Pokémon Company International.
©1995–2018 Nintendo / Creatures Inc. / GAME FREAK inc.
TM, ®, and character names are trademarks of Nintendo.
POCKET MONSTERS SPECIAL SUN • MOON Vol. 2
by Hidenori KUSAKA, Satoshi YAMAMOTO
© 2017 Hidenori KUSAKA, Satoshi YAMAMOTO
All rights reserved.
Original Japanese edition published by SHOGAKUKAN.
English translation rights in the United States of America, Canada, the United Kingdom,
Ireland, Australia, New Zealand and India arranged with SHOGAKUKAN.

Original Cover Design—Hiroyuki KAWASOME (grafio)

English Adaptation—Bryant Turnage
Translation—Tetsuichiro Miyaki
Touch-Up & Lettering—Susan Daigle-Leach
Design—Alice Lewis
Editor—Annette Roman

Printed in the U.S.A.

Published by
VIZ Media, LLC
P.O. Box 77010
San Francisco, CA 94107

10 9 8 7 6 5 4 3 2 1
First printing, January 2019

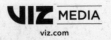
viz.com

Coming Next Volume

Volume 4

Will Sun ever learn to master the Z-Move? Several obstacles stand in his way. Trial Captain Kiawe might be able to teach him, but first Sun and Moon have to rescue him from a Team Skull attack! Then Sun has to get his hands on a Z-Ring. And if he manages all that, he still has to prove his mettle to Island Guardian Tapu Lele!

And will Sun successfully deliver his order of special berries?

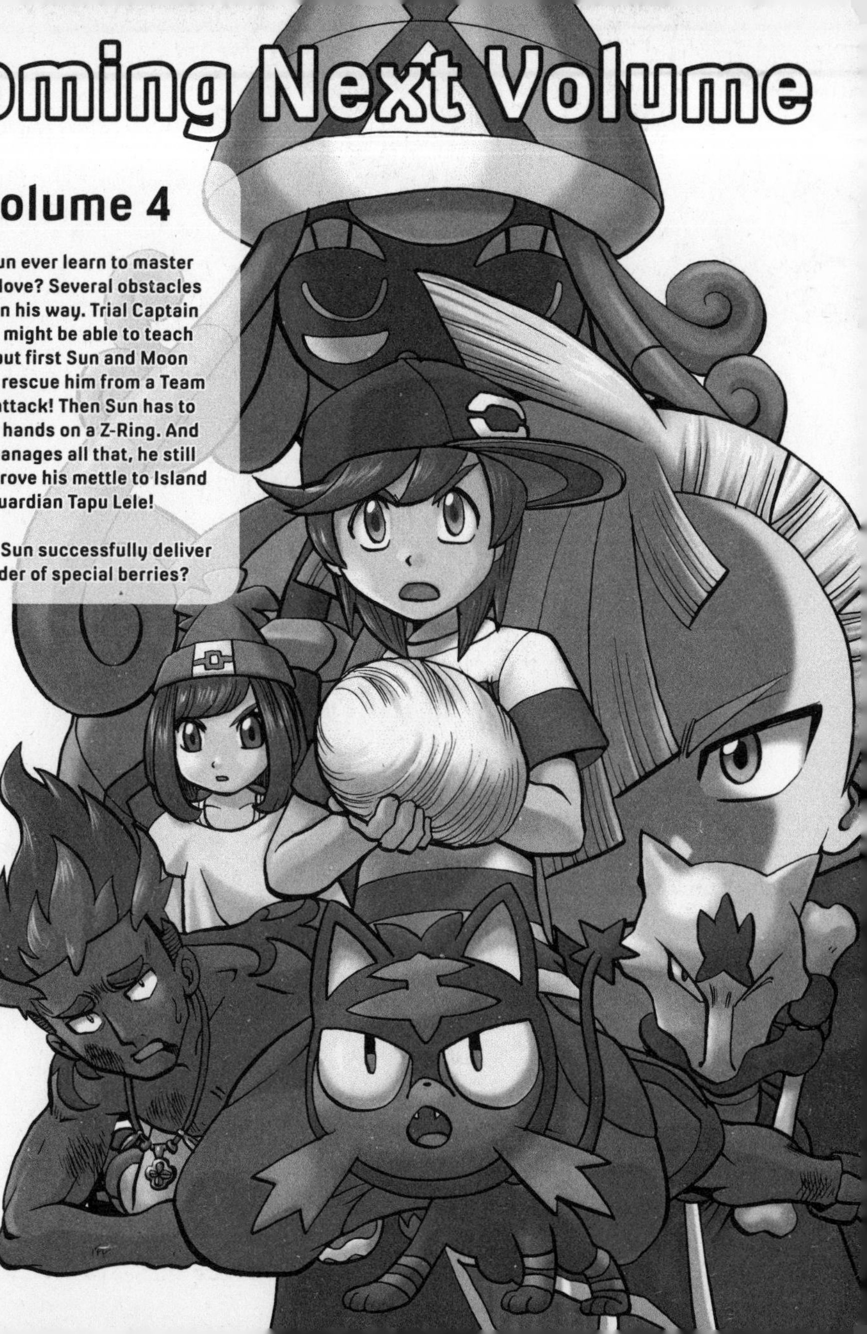

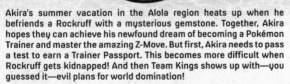

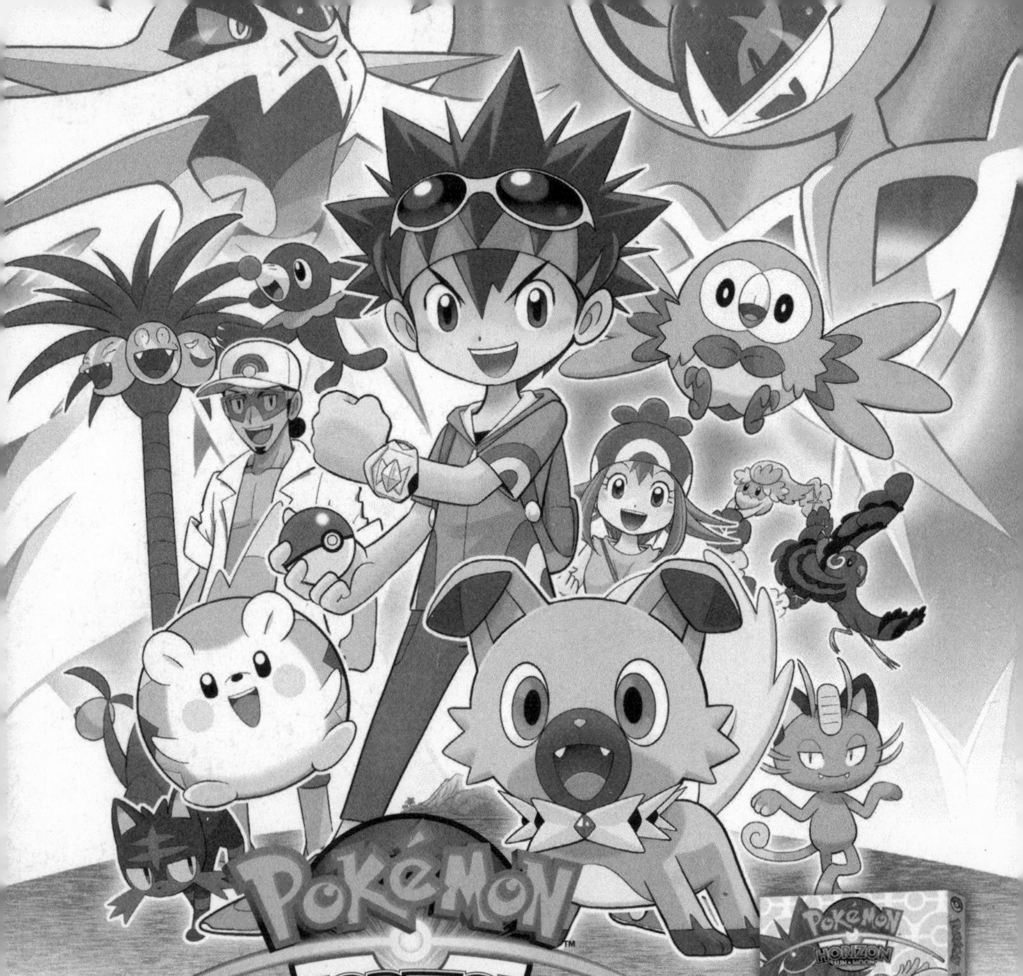

Pokémon

HORIZON
SUN & MOON

Akira's summer vacation in the Alola region heats up when he befriends a Rockruff with a mysterious gemstone. Together, Akira hopes they can achieve his newfound dream of becoming a Pokémon Trainer and master the amazing Z-Move. But first, Akira needs to pass a test to earn a Trainer Passport. This becomes more difficult when Rockruff gets kidnapped! And then Team Kings shows up with—you guessed it—evil plans for world domination!

Story & Art
TENYA YABUNO

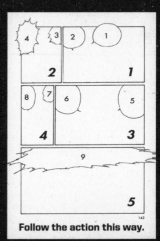

YOU'RE READING THE WRONG WAY! THIS IS THE END OF THIS GRAPHIC NOVEL!

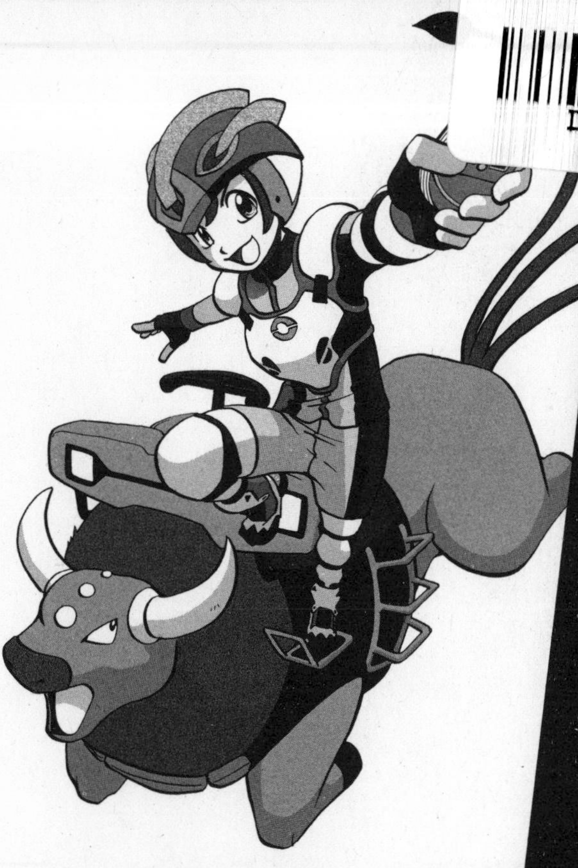

To properly enjoy this VIZ Media graphic novel, please turn it around and begin reading from right to left.

This book has been printed in the original Japanese format in order to preserve the orientation of the original artwork. Have fun with it!

<<< READ THIS WAY!

Follow the action this way.